Sadyra

Book 2 of the Banebridge Companion Novels

A Story in the Soul Forge Universe

Sadyra by Richard H. Stephens

www.richardhstephens.com

Cover & interior art by: Widget Wyvern Studios
Paperback ISBN: 978-1-989257-24-1

2nd Edition: 2021

Acknowledgements

Sadyra is the second of three books in the Banebridge Companion Novels; complementing the first book, *Larina*.

While looking to fill in the time between the completion of the Legends of the Lurker series and a research trip* to the British Isles, I wanted to do something different. I surveyed my amazing readers and asked them which minor character from either of my first two series would they like to read about. Sadyra, the cheeky, fun loving, wear her heart on her sleeve archer from the Soul Forge Saga was the winner. She beat out notables, Olmar, another favourite from the Soul Forge Saga, and Devius Misenthorpe and Tamra Stoneheart, from the Legends of the Lurker series. I thoroughly enjoyed fleshing out the backstories that explain how Sadyra and Larina came to fight alongside Pollard Banebridge in the Splendoor Catacombs Guard—a division of the Songsbirthian Guard.

*Unfortunately, my research trip has been cancelled due to COVID-19, so the Rise of Grimclaw is now on hold.

On the bright side, as one good thing comes to a halt, another opportunity arises. I am excited to announce the next series in the Soul Forge Universe: The Draakvarian Chronicles. This series will revolve around the elves, Ouderling Wys and Pecklyn Ors, filling in the history with regard to the emergence of the Windwalkers.

Sadyra is dedicated to everyone in the world who has selflessly kept our world running while it fell apart around us. The words, ‘thank you,’ seem so inadequate in expressing our heartfelt appreciation.

None of these stories would be possible without the input of my incredible beta readers. A heartfelt thank you to: Joshua Stephens, Paul Stephens, Alyssa Gelata, and of course, Caroline Davidson, who is always in the trenches alongside me.

I would also like to extend a big thank you to my cover and interior picture designer, Tessa Escalera at Widget Wyvern Studios.

Special credit: To honour the Indigenous Peoples of North America, I chose the name Lozen to represent an Altirius Mountain Indian; a title that appears in the original book, *Soul Forge*. All incidents involving Lozen in the books, *Larina*, and *Sadyra*, and *Pollard* are purely fictitious, and by no means represent the real warrior, Lozen.

A brief, unverified history of Lozen.

A famous warrior and prophet of the Chihenne Chiricahua Apache, Lozen was the sister of Chief Victorio.

Born in the 1840s, her brother once said, *"Lozen is my right hand...strong as a man, braver than most, and cunning in strategy. Lozen is a shield to her people."*

Lozen used her spiritual powers in battle; calling on the favour of the gods to discover the location and movement of the enemy.

She participated in many fights on the San Carlos Reservation in Arizona. During those fights, she helped many women and children escape the hands of the enemy and avoided capture herself.

A warrior named Kaywaykla, once said, "She could ride, shoot, and fight like a man; and I think she had more ability in planning military strategy than Victorio."

Lozen fought alongside Geronimo in the last campaign of the Apache Wars.

Going forward.

As in my last series, The Legends of the Lurker, I will be searching for new and unique dragon names. If you wish to submit a name to be added to my list, please connect with me on my Facebook Author Page: RichardHughStephens

Credit in the form of a personal thank you, in the foreword of the book in which the names are used, is my way of giving back to you, the reader. (Including your real name in the acknowledgements will only occur with your permission.)

Zephyr
The Unknown Sea
Mt. Cinder
Mt. Gloom
Cliff Face
Altirius Mountains
Dragonfang Pass
Fishmonger Bay
Thunderhead
Storms End
Madrigail Bay
The Forke
Frothe River
Redfire Path
The Slither
Zephyr Flats
Castle Svelte
Carillon
Ring Lake
Saros' Swamp
Forbidden Swamp
West Castle Rd
Millsford Rd
Madrigail R.
Millsford
Canorous River
Alpheus' Arch
St. Carmichael's Shrine
Madrigail Lake
Splendor Falls
Songsbirth
The Muse
The Spine
Olde Gritian Rd
Gritian Hills
Niad Ocean
Torpid Marsh
Gritian
Trencher's Gorge
Undying Wall
Forbidden Pass
Lowland Grasslands
The Gulch
Nordic Woods
Nordic Town
Redfire Path
The Ocean Way
Apexceal
Ember Breath
Ghost Island
N

Table of Contents

Mysterious Cabin on the Hill 1

Capsized 19

Wrecked 36

Gitch 47

The Crew 65

Scourge of the Catch 74

Witch's Cauldron 80

Seaside Antics 98

Learning the Ropes 105

Going Home 113

One of the Crew 119

If Only 127

The Reckoning 141

Tougher than Life 148

To Live Another Day 157

To Catch a Tiger 165

Kindred Spirits 174

To view the full colour maps in the Soul Forge Universe, please visit: www.richardhstephens.com

Sadyra

Book 2 of the Banebridge Companion Novels

A Story in the Soul Forge Universe

Sadyra

Mysterious Cabin on the Hill

There was something mysterious about the cabin on the hill—something sinister, if Sadyra cared to dwell on it. She didn't. She had suffered too many sleepless nights worrying about the rumours whispered in her presence whenever she visited the village of Fishmonger Bay sprawled at the bottom of the hill. The backwater village rife with rumours concerning the shack she called home.

Standing at the end of a path that led away from her family's dilapidated hut, she examined the coastline spread out far below; jagged reefs relentlessly pummeled by ocean swells. Her gaze followed the main trail down a steep slope in the opposite direction of Fishmonger Bay to where it connected with the shoreline and continued northward beneath a promontory of black rock projecting over the ocean at a dizzying height. The Summoning Stone.

She shivered. There was something ominous about that large, flat rock. Perhaps its name. Why would anyone summon anything out there? If there was a place in Zephyr farther away from meaningful civilization, she didn't know of one.

And yet, every three years during the spring equinox, people migrated to the Summoning Stone to take part in a bizarre celebration known as the Mating Festival.

Mesmerized by the relentless waves crashing against the reef, Sadyra shivered. It was high summer, two years after the last gathering, and already she had witnessed the heightened activity surrounding next year's festivities.

She cringed. The hedonistic rituals performed during the weeklong Mating Festival had always repulsed her. Ever since she could remember, her parents had dragged her and her younger sisters to watch the barbaric rituals unfold—all in some bizarre act to appease the dragon gods. Every festival except the last.

The Mating Festival was a time of coming together for the hardy people eking out a meagre living on the rugged shores of the Niad Ocean. Fishermen mostly. The dangerous shoals abutting the coastline around Fishmonger Bay provided those tough enough to live here an abundant supply of fish with which to trade in larger cities like Thunderhead and Storms End, many leagues to the south.

For most of its residents, Fishmonger Bay provided a haven from society—harbouring those seeking refuge from people who might take exception to their past deeds should they ever run into them again.

To Sadyra, the backwater village was a dead-end place to live. Unless, of course, one was content to work themselves from sunup to sundown, breaking their back in hopes of reaping the puny rewards their catch might net them from the skinflint buyers in the big city. Not to mention the ever-present danger of plying one's trade along the razor-sharp reefs lining the northwestern coast of Zephyr. A danger Sadyra was all too familiar with.

Many were the evenings Sadyra's father would stumble into their hut, stone drunk and babbling about the latest victim of the surf. Those days were mostly behind him now. It was Sadyra's turn to brave the unpredictable ocean currents and provide for the household—allowing him and her mother more time to maintain their constant state of semi-consciousness.

Brought up to be a hard worker, Sadyra had done as she had been instructed for as long as she could remember; mending nets, gutting fish, and hauling backbreaking buckets laden with the day's catch from her father's leaky dory to the warehouse fronting the rickety pier. She had learned the value of a hard day's effort, and the daily routine had conditioned her to maintain the rigours of working on the ocean.

Being the eldest child, Sadyra knew nothing else. Up before dawn, expected to prepare breakfast—one her parents would inevitably complain about—and then off to the village to assist her father. Day in and day out, she lugged the family's scant fishing gear down the steep trail into Fishmonger Bay, to where their poor excuse of a boat lay on the gravelly beach.

Every now and then, as they worked the ocean swells, the miserable man would look at her and grumble something about a reckoning. She had no idea what that meant but judging by his scowl, whatever it was, it had to be her fault.

A hand clamped on her shoulder. "Nice view."

Sadyra jumped and reached for the filleting knife tucked in its worn sheath at her waist but the hand stayed her arm.

She swallowed, knowing the voice all too well. Bano Shell. The young man her parents had betrothed her to in the spring. The man with whom she would be expected to take part in next year's Mating Festival.

Sadyra cursed the day she had, in her mother's words, blossomed. At seventeen, her womanly physique had filled out quicker than other girls her age, making her popular with the boys. An attribute she wasn't keen on. Other than her wish to someday get out from underneath the life sucking pall of her parents, she wanted nothing more than to be left alone.

The advent of Bano Shell's betrothal had gone a long way to keeping other suitors away, but Sadyra wasn't convinced that was a good thing.

Faking a smile; dimples lifted her freckled cheeks. "It's beautiful."

"I'd say."

She sighed. Bano's eyes weren't looking at the scenery. Shrugging free of his grasp, she waited until his dull, brown gaze met hers.

He raised his eyebrows suggestively. "Tural give you the day off?"

"Couldn't drag himself out of bed, more like."

"Again?"

"What else is new?"

"I guess it's no big deal. You're running the boat on your own most days now, aren't you?"

"Pretty much." She looked away. Her voice dropped to a whisper. "I hit a reef yesterday."

"Oh, oh."

She nodded. "Capsized, too. Had to swim it back to shore."

"Much damage?"

"I'll say. That's why I'm standing here. I need Father's help to fix it."

Bano looked up the path leading to Sadyra's hut and said under his breath, "Lose much?"

"The whole lot."

"And?"

Sadyra fought off tears. She pulled the waistband of her breeks down her hip and lifted her shift part way up her back, exposing a series of deep bruises.

"From the shoals?"

Sadyra shook her head.

"Oh Sadie. I'm sorry."

Sadyra swallowed. Steeling her emotions, she stared at the raging surf breaking over the reefs far below. She didn't appreciate Bano calling her by her nickname. Only people she considered friends were allowed to call her Sadie. "Ain't your fault."

"True, but you shouldn't get beaten for an act of nature."

"Ya, try telling him that. He says I need to keep my mind on what I'm about, not where I want to be. If I paid better attention, I would've seen the reef before I struck it."

Sadyra

"The sea was angry yesterday. You had no business being out there. My father spent the day tending his nets."

Sadyra grimaced. "Ya? Well, according to *my* father, it's my duty to earn me and my sisters' keep. At least until they're old enough to join me."

"Sleena's old enough. What is she? Twelve?"

"Ten."

"Weren't you fishing with your father before then?"

"Oh, aye. I can remember dragging the buckets across the shore. They were half as big as me."

"Why doesn't she help?"

Sadyra shrugged. "Don't know. Father's got a sweet spot for her."

"What about…?" Bano's brow furrowed.

"Sable?"

"Yes, Sable."

It was useless trying to figure out her parents' motivations. "Who knows? If anything, Father detests Sable more than me."

"Come on. It can't be that bad."

Sadyra glowered at him until he broke eye contact.

He shook his head. "And he hasn't said anything more to you about your ancestors?"

Her breath caught. Her family history was a sore point with her parents, and Bano knew it. He had convinced her to inquire about it a few months ago and she had been beaten unconscious as a result.

She glared at Bano and noticed what appeared to be the hilt of a priceless dagger protruding from an ancient sheath attached to his belt. "Where'd you get that?"

He followed her gaze. "Huh? Oh, that? It's nothing, really. Just something my parents gave me."

"Looks expensive."

"Bah. Appearances can be deceiving."

She thought he seemed embarrassed. "Hmm. Well, anyway, I don't care to discuss my father, okay?"

Bano nodded, letting it go. His gaze lingered on the two small headstones barely visible amongst the undergrowth—their amateurish inscriptions no longer legible.

Shaking her head at the impetuous man's fascination with her family heritage, she sat down on the brink of the steep drop-off to await her father.

The sound of a door squealing and banging made Sadyra cringe. Tural Ors was awake.

Bano had grown bored with Sadyra and returned to the village a while ago. She didn't blame him. She wasn't good company today.

Rising to her feet, she looked at the ground as her father lumbered down the path. Stepping onto the main trail, he grunted and made his way toward Fishmonger Bay.

Sadyra fell in behind, mindful to keep her distance lest her presence awaken his latest irritation with her.

The sleepy village of Fishmonger Bay was built in a small clearing at the base of Peril's Peak—the mountain's permanently snow-capped summit sparkling in the afternoon sunshine.

She had climbed those heights on many occasions as a child to escape the wrath of her parents. Two years ago, just before the Mating Festival, she had fled there with her younger sisters to keep them from harm's way. Her parents had indulged in a drunken bender worse than any she could remember. Fearing the outcome, as these episodes never ended well, she snuck Sleena and Sable away from the hut and led them to an abandoned cabin high upon Peril's Peak.

Sadyra had been fourteen then; her sister Sleena, eight, and Sable, five. It wasn't lost on Sadyra that their birth years coincided with the Mating Festival. Nor could she forget the day she had brought her sisters home; weary, starving, and afraid. It had taken her a good month before the resulting injuries of her disobedience allowed her to sleep through the night. It had been a lesson she wouldn't soon forget.

Watching the slumped shoulders of her downtrodden father crunching across the gravel common area between the buildings lining the base of the mountain and the warehouse dominating the shore, Sadyra found herself feeling sorry for him. As much as she hated the sight of the grizzled, pepper-grey haired man, she knew deep down there had to be an underlying reason for his perpetual malaise. One that he blamed her and her sisters for.

Many of the villagers shunned Tural Ors. Upon seeing him, they would change direction and avoid having any dealings with the man. Sadyra had always thought it was largely due to her father's mean streak, but lately she had begun to rethink her views on *both* of her parents' mannerisms.

Feeding on Bano's peculiar interest into her family's past, she started to wonder whether something deeper and darker lie at the root of her parents' troubles. She wished there was someone she could speak to but it was a touchy subject to bring up. It wouldn't end well if her inquiries made it back to her parents. She couldn't afford to spend time recovering if she wished to keep deflecting their everlasting anger from her sisters.

Tural stopped and stared at the damaged boat. Hands on hips, he shook his head and grumbled.

Sadyra couldn't make out what he said, nor did she want to know. Whatever it was, was no doubt directed at her.

She took a deep breath and looked around, hopeful to see other villagers in case he went off. She grunted. Even had there been anyone close by, their presence wouldn't make a difference. Though not the biggest man in the village, she doubted anyone was brave enough to challenge Tural when he was in one of his moods. It was all she could do not to run away as his dark gaze turned on her.

"Where's the rest of the boat?"

She swallowed. The surf pounded the shoreline. Curling waves rose above a ramshackle jetty that extended into the brine. She forced a smile and shrugged, trying to ease the tension with a high-pitched voice. "Out there somewhere?"

Tural followed her gaze. He took a couple of deep breaths. "Your mama's gonna be livid if we don't make this week's quota."

More like, Mama's gonna be angry she can't afford enough grog to keep her pickled, Sadyra thought. Had it been anyone else facing her, she would have voiced her feelings. But not her father. She had enough bruises.

"I reckon you best head into the mountain and fetch us some grub while I see if I can repair this tub."

"Yes, Father."

"It ain't to be pretty, I can tell you that." He shook his head as he examined the damage. "Next time you hit a reef, you best pray your head's between the boat and the rock."

She bit her lips, fighting the angry rebuttal that demanded release; the hurt evident in her soft answer. "Yes, Father."

Bano must have been watching for Sadyra because he caught up to her as she crunched across the commons and slipped between two buildings to gain the trailhead.

"Wait up."

Sadyra stopped, her shoulders stiffening. She rolled her eyes before turning to meet his approach. A forced smile briefly crossed her face. She wanted to be left alone.

"How'd it go?"

She shrugged. "He didn't hit me again, if that's what you're asking?"

"I know. I mean, what did he say?"

So, he *had* been watching. "Not much. Said it was my fault."

She looked toward the ocean swells so Bano wouldn't see her struggling to keep from crying. Her father's words echoed in her mind, *'Next time you hit a reef, you best pray your head's between the boat and the rock.'*

Taking a deep breath, she turned to Bano and lifted her eyebrows. "Father wants me to hunt while he mends the boat."

"I'll grab my bow and go with you."

Not waiting for a reply, he spun around and jogged into the village.

Sadyra sighed but waited for his return.

Bano on her heels, she climbed the foothill to where a smaller path veered toward her family's cabin. She couldn't help but look at the two grave markers hidden amongst the undergrowth. She had never given them much thought before. They had always been there. They were part of the familiar landscape; just as the mountain slope climbing high above their hut, or the dark promontory projecting from the cliffs beyond the foothill.

She took a couple of steps up the side path but Bano's voice stopped her.

"Don't you ever wonder who they were?"

She didn't have to turn around to know who he was talking about. Following his gaze as he crouched and parted the grasses around the granite markers—the eroded inscriptions covered in lichen—he ran a hand over one of the gravestones.

"No. Not really. Father says they were distant relatives from centuries ago."

Bano nodded. "And that doesn't interest you?"

"Why should it? I never knew them."

Bano straightened and faced her, his usual smugness absent. "You do know the history behind the cabin you live in, don't you?"

Sadyra shrugged. "Ya. Kind of. Don't really care, to be honest. I'm just counting the days until I can get away from here."

"I don't blame you."

Sadyra thought he was referring to her treatment at the hands of her parents but his next words surprised her.

"A witch used to live in your cabin. A family of them."

She scrunched her eyebrows. She had heard something to that effect a few times over the years, but hadn't paid any attention to it. The residents of Fishmonger Bay had nothing better to do once the catch was brought in than tell tall tales of people they had heard about. As a young girl, she had been as frightened by the stories as the next child, but like everything in the forsaken village, nothing was what it seemed. She had had a hard time differentiating truth from folklore until she started hanging out with the older children.

"So I've been told."

"You don't believe it?"

"Doesn't matter what I believe. That was a long time ago. It has nothing to do with me."

"But it does." Bano's eyes grew wide. He pointed a dirty fingernail at her. "According to Father Cloth, that hut has been in your family for over five hundred years."

He nodded as Sadyra frowned.

"Aye. Back to the time of the Dragon Witch."

Sadyra held his stare and swallowed.

"That means you're related—"

"Pfft!" Sadyra scowled and stormed up the path. "Doesn't mean anything. It's a rumour to scare children into staying off the mountain to save them from the trolls."

Bano breathed heavily behind her as he tried to keep up—a small hut appearing at the end of the path. "So, you're calling Father Cloth a liar?"

Sadyra stopped abruptly and spun on him, her finger in *his* face. "I never said that. I said I don't believe what everyone says."

"What? You don't believe in magic?"

The question quenched her rising anger. She took a couple of deep breaths. "I've never met anyone capable of doing anything out of the ordinary. Have you?"

"No but…What about the sorcerer who almost seized the Ivory Throne a couple years back? Surely Queen Quarrnaine didn't give her life to defend the realm from a commoner."

"That's different."

"How?"

"I don't know. Just is. That man came from across the ocean."

"That *man*? His name was Helleden Misenthorpe. People claim he descended from the Wizard of the North."

Sadyra shook her head, tired of the conversation. Bano was speaking in riddles. She had no idea who this northern wizard was, nor did she care. "Whatever. It doesn't matter. Yes, I'll admit there used to be magic users in Zephyr, but from what Father tells me, there aren't anymore."

"Sadyra! What are you doing here? You're supposed to helping your father."

Sadyra rolled her eyes for Bano's benefit and turned to see her mother hanging onto the doorjamb of their one-roomed hut for support. Not even midafternoon and the sour-faced woman was heavy into the spirits.

"It's okay, Mother. Father told me to hunt until he gets it repaired."

Her mother, Areeza Ors, scowled, her weathered face wrinkled well beyond her years. The villagers often remarked how much Sadyra looked like her mother, but Sadyra couldn't see it. She hoped she didn't look anything like the old hag.

Areeza's glassy stare found Bano, as if just realizing he was behind Sadyra. Her face lit up. "Oh! Bano. What a pleasant surprise." Areeza primped her rat's nest—traces of auburn struggling to coexist with mid back length grey strands.

Bano puffed out his chest. “Hi, Mrs. Ors. You’re looking swell as ever.”

“Och. You’re such a flatterer.”

Sadyra glared at Bano and said under her breath so only he could hear, “Really?” She shook her head and twisted to slip past her mother into the dingy hut.

Sable and Sleena looked up from the sewing they were doing at the dinner table, their dirty faces following her to the small space the three of them shared at night in the back corner of the cabin on the far side of a cluttered counter.

Retrieving her crude bow hung on a couple of pegs, she found her protective leather forearm sleeves, snatched up her half empty quiver, and stormed from the hut.

She didn’t bother looking at her mother, but Areeza’s voice followed her around the back of the cabin, “See to it you get one with meat on it this time. The one you brought back the other day could barely feed a chicken.”

Biting back an angry retort, Sadyra stomped across the backyard.

“Sadie, slow down,” Bano protested, his gear rattling.

She stopped where the mountainside shot steeply up—its upper heights disappearing beyond an inaccessible ridge—and gave him a dark look. “If you see magic in that woman, you’re as drunk as she is.”

Candles of varying height flickered around the musty interior of the Ors’ family hut—the evening darkness masking the filth and clutter.

Sadyra sat beside her youngest sister, Sable. The skinny whelp nestled into Sadyra’s side—more to get away from the sour smell of their mother’s breath and her surly looks than to be close to Sadyra.

Sadyra didn't mind. The two shared a special bond. She understood Sable's feelings better than anyone. Other than the times Sadyra took a beating to save her sisters from their parents' wrath, there wasn't an occasion she despised more than gathering for the evening meal.

Sleena sat across the table, minding her own business, but she needn't fear. For the most part, their parents left her alone. Why, Sadyra had no idea. She found herself happy for Sleena and jealous at the same time. Whatever the reason, it wasn't Sleena's fault.

To break the monotonous, brooding silence that gripped every dinnertime, Sadyra said between mouthfuls of venison—part of the catch her mother had complained about earlier. "Do you think there are any magic users left in the world?"

Tural exchanged looks with Areeza before staring hard at Sadyra. "Why do you ask?"

Not sure whether to continue, Sadyra thought, *why not*? It had been Bano's idea anyway, and they loved the cretin.

"I don't know. Something Bano said."

Her parents waited for her to continue.

Sleena stopped eating and watched with interest.

Sable snuggled into Sadyra as if trying to disappear.

Sadyra wrapped a comforting arm around her little sister and examined the slovenly cabin. "Bano said this used to be a witch's hut."

Tural frowned.

"He thinks we might be related to the..." Sadyra swallowed at the dark glares she received from her parents—her last words coming out as no more than a whisper, "...Dragon Witch."

Tural stiffened and stared hard at Sadyra, his face unreadable. Putting down his well-honed knife with the greatest of care, he wiped his lips on his cuff. His chair scraped on the wooden floorboards as he rose to his feet.

Sadyra felt Sable tremble against her.

Sleena bowed her head, not daring to look at either of their parents.

They all knew by their father's mannerism what was about to happen.

"Outside with you," was all he said before he stomped across the hut and threw the door open to the night.

Sadyra looked from Sleena to their mother and sighed. She had the uncanny knack of igniting her father's anger.

Resigned to the fact that she had no choice but to obey, Sadyra swallowed what was left in her mouth, took a sip of water from an old, wooden cup, and followed her father into the darkness.

He waited for her on the end of the rotting porch fronting the hut—its sagging boards in dire need of replacing.

"In the back," Tural grunted.

Not waiting, he disappeared behind the cabin. She contemplated bolting down the path, but she had nowhere to go. The hunting cabin up by the summit was the only place she could think of. Her father would look there first.

She was confident she could get to the old cabin long before he would—a day at least, as she had discovered a back route that no one else seemed aware of. That, however, would only intensify the violence her father would hand out. One of these days, she feared he would kill her.

It took every ounce of strength she had to walk down the porch and into the backyard to where Tural waited with hands on hips, refusing to look at her.

She followed his gaze to the full moon—its face partially obscured by a thin veil of cloud.

"What am I to do with you?"

Sadyra didn't trust herself to speak. She interlaced her thin fingers and stared at them clasped together beside the sheath holding her filleting knife.

A dark thought seeped into her mind. It would be too easy to stick him with it. Over and over again until his ridicule and vile ways lay dead at her feet.

She shivered. Where had that come from? She couldn't seriously consider such an action…Could she?

She bit on her lips and forced her gaze to settle on her father's unshaven face. His once chiselled features had sagged over the years—distorted by deep lines and extra weight. Recalling how he looked years ago, she might have considered him handsome once upon a time. But not now. Not with her knowledge of who he really was. A drunken letch who resorted to violence whenever life didn't go as he thought it should. That happened most days now that Sadyra had grown up.

Tural fixed her with that evil glare of his, his dark eyes narrowed beneath heavy brows.

Sadyra flinched and cowered, expecting the inevitable, but Tural crossed thick, hairy forearms on top of his protruding stomach.

"What do you know of magic?"

Surprised, Sadyra gulped, her voice meek. "Nothing, Father. Just what I hear from my friends and Father Cloth."

"Have you felt anything unusual stir inside you?"

Sadyra squinted, trying to find relevance in the odd question. She thought of Bano and felt like spitting. "Not at all. Bano and I have never…" She didn't know how to finish the sentence in an acceptable manner.

"I didn't ask if you were pregnant." Tural tilted his head. "Are you?"

"No!" Sadyra spit out harsher than was wise, but he didn't appear to take exception to her tone.

"That's good. That's the last thing your mother and I need right now."

You and mother? What about me? she thought, but kept it to herself.

He stepped up to her and grabbed her shoulders in his large hands, painfully squeezing as he stared into her eyes. "I mean, have you noticed anything *different* inside? Something weird or foreign to anything you're used to?"

Sadyra swallowed. His grip made her squirm under its pressure but she knew better than to pull away. Wild thoughts raced through her mind as she tried to make sense of his question. "You mean my moon flow?"

He shook her hard—her head whipped back and forth. "No, you dolt! Are you experiencing anything *magical*?"

She couldn't respond until her head stopped shaking. Her scared eyes found his. "No, Father? Why would you ask something like that?"

He shook her again; not as hard this time. "Think! Have you noticed anything out of the ordinary? Like, how you survived the shipwreck when the boat was damaged almost beyond repair? Did you do something a normal person couldn't?"

She remembered the boat being carried on the tidal surges into the reefs. No amount of rowing had been able to avert the water's pull once it had the boat in its clutches. If anything, it was chance that had saved her. Just before the boat hit the shoal, the undertow had exposed the jagged reef. Without thinking, she had jumped over the side of the boat into the heavy surf. The next surge had lifted her over the razor-sharp ridge of stone and deposited her and the remains of the boat on its far side.

"No, Father. I was lucky, I guess. One moment I was rowing for my life, and the next, I was in the water."

His fingers tightened on her shoulders.

She feared he would separate her muscles from the bone. She involuntarily tried to pull away. "Ow! You're hurting me."

He shoved her backward and let go.

She tried to catch herself with several quick backsteps but couldn't help falling on her backside.

Tural stood over her.

She prepared to feel the toe of his boot, but it didn't come.

Tural let out a long breath. "Lucky? Pfft. Weren't lucky for me or your mother."

Sadyra pondered what that meant. She knew all too well that her father would rather she had hit the reef instead of the boat.

He started to walk away but stopped. Without looking back, he said, “If you ever mention the Dragon Witch again, I’ll dash your head off the reef myself.”

A dark rage festered in Sadyra. She was tempted to get up off the ground and drive her dagger into his back. Gaining her feet, she fought to steady her breathing and glared at his receding form; unabashedly wishing he’d drop dead on the spot.

Her blood ran cold as he stopped at the corner of the hut and turned—shadows casting his features in an evil light.

“You’d best be making up for your mistake tomorrow. Or perhaps you’d rather I put your mongrel to work.”

Sadyra’s eyes widened. “No. Please. Sable’s too young. I’ll do better, I promise.”

He held her gaze as if searching her soul. “See that you do, else she’ll be taking your place, you hear?”

Sadyra swallowed at the inference. If something happened to her, her youngest sister would bear the brunt of their parents’ unhappiness. That scared her more than any threat of being beaten.

For some reason Areeza despised Sable almost as much as her. Their father had mentioned Sable looked just like their mother when Areeza was good looking. Before Sadyra had come along and ruined their mother’s body.

As her mind returned to the present, she realized her father had gone. Tears dribbled down her cheeks but she didn’t care. They fueled her resolve. She would do better tomorrow. Much better. If everything went as she hoped, she could pocket a little coin herself. That was her goal. Work harder than ever before and keep a little for herself—saving it until she had enough to take her sisters away from here. Out of harm’s way.

She wasn't concerned about Sleena at the moment, but if she left Sleena behind, their parents would have no one else to vent on. It might do her middle sister some good to see how she and Sable were treated, but in her heart, Sadyra would never do that to her.

She kicked at a half-submerged stone in the grass, dislodging it from a pocket of dirt. Picking it up, she threw it at the back of the cabin; wincing as it almost struck the lone window. If the glass had shattered, so would her body—at the hands of her parents.

Swallowing the bitterness, she trembled with anger at her helplessness. Teeth clenched, she promised herself that someday soon, she and her sisters would be free of the mysterious cabin on the hill. When that happened, she would never go by the family name, Ors, again.

Sadyra

Capsized

Ocean swells higher than Sadyra was tall made it difficult to keep the bow of the leaking rowboat on a southerly tack. Sadyra's hands ached from pulling on the oars but the pain was little compared to that in her shoulders—her right one especially as the rugged shoreline slipped past excruciatingly slow.

She drew from a deep reserve she never knew she possessed—driven by the fact that the day's catch exceeded anything she had ever brought in before. Facing the rear of the boat to ply the oars, if she craned her neck, the distant skyline of Thundcrhcad was visiblc whenever the rowboat crested a high swell.

Despite her discomfort, the corners of her thin lips turned up in a satisfied grin. She would fetch enough with the day's catch that she could provide her parents with more than they were used to and still hold back some for herself.

The sprawling squalor of thc northern edge of Thunderhead slid past. Soon, the lesser quays of the smaller fish merchants littered the shoreline. The more affluent businesses, where the bigger fishing boats sold their catch, were protected within the fjord farther south, but she didn't care. That only meant more rowing.

With practised ease, she timed the swells and angled her little craft toward the dilapidated wharf the individual fishermen from Fishmonger Bay used to sell their fish.

A teenaged boy, Sadyra knew as Swab, ran across the dock clad in nothing but shin length, tan breeks—their colour not as dark as the skinny boy's skin. Not much older than thirteen or fourteen, a great smile lifted his cheeks on seeing who was plying the oars.

"Sadyra! You're back. How's the haul?"

Sadyra rolled her eyes, but she didn't let Swab see her do so. She didn't appreciate how he fawned over her, but the awkward boy meant well. Ignoring his question, she scrambled to untangle the bow rope while preventing the rough surf from smashing her boat into the pier.

"Wow. Looks like you had a great day." Swab caught the wildly thrown rope and braced his slight frame to help Sadyra control her boat. He flicked a lock of curly, dirty-blonde hair from his face and tugged hard before wrapping the rope around a rusted iron hook embedded in the thick planks of the jetty. Three quick wraps and a deft hitch knot, and Swab stood waiting to catch the stern hawser.

Sadyra pitched it to him and braced her hands against the side of the waterlogged dock, careful not to pinch her fingers as the next swell threatened to pull the stern away.

Whatever she thought about the dockhand, she couldn't deny his expertise at securing small boats in the face of heavy seas.

The boat secure, he held out his hand.

She accepted his callused grip and hopped onto the jetty—immediately facing the shore and bracing herself as a large wave broke over the pier, drenching them—their hands still bound.

Swab shook out his dripping locks as if nothing had happened, and shyly released her hand. "Come. Get yourself dried off and talk to Skipper. I'll get you unloaded."

Not waiting for a reply, he jogged the length of the jetty and snatched up several rope baskets piled against the wet wall of the one-story warehouse that sat behind a row of jagged, black rock where the ocean swells met landfall.

Sadyra walked toward the warehouse; moving aside as Swab bustled about his business. He dropped the baskets on the edge of the dock except for the one he took with him into her boat and began collecting the catch piled in the scuppers.

A solid wood door squealed on rusted hinges as Sadyra pushed her way into the cramped office of the 'North Shore Fishery.'

A bald man with an ample stomach gazed at her through the smoky pall suspended in the air. The bowl of his pipe brightened and another waft of smoke escaped his pale lips to comingle with the cloud. He lifted a thick eyebrow. "Ors. Missed you the last couple of days. Thought the kraken had taken ya."

"Humph. More like the reefs, Skipper."

Skipper leaned forward. "Much damage?"

"Father fixed it."

Skipper leaned back and lifted both eyebrows. "Bet that didn't go over well."

"Not really." She unconsciously rubbed at her hidden bruises.

"I can only imagine."

The gruff owner almost sounded like he commiserated with her, but it was tough to see beyond his hardened expression.

"Mind if I…" Sadyra left the last words unspoken, but Skipper nodded.

Squeezing through the cluttered office, Sadyra pushed open the rear door and entered the warehouse proper.

Several sets of eyes looked up from where they bent over low benches; digging at shells and filleting the bigger fish lying about. The stench of the large room turned up her nostrils. She couldn't imagine how these people did this day in and day out.

Upon reaching the tiny room set aside for people to relieve their bladder, Sadyra looked through the cracks in the thin wall to make sure nobody was close by.

By the time she returned to the office, Swab was talking to Skipper.

Swab's face lit up as she entered but Skipper cleared his throat and Swab slipped through the outer door without a word.

"Nice haul, Ors."

Sadyra bristled at the continued mention of her last name but knew better than to complain.

Skipper pushed several coins across the desktop. "That's one of the better hauls today."

Sadyra gaped at the coins. There were barely more than she usually received.

Skipper must've noticed her consternation. "What?" He growled. "Do you not agree with your settlement?"

There were many things she wanted to say. She wanted to tell the arrogant man that she was tired of being cheated out of the rate he paid the *fishermen*. Just because she was a girl didn't mean her fish were worth any less. Taking a deep breath, she swallowed. "No sir."

"Good. I'd hate to be forced to send you elsewhere. The markets are volatile this time of the year. With the glut of summer fish, I'll be lucky if I don't take a loss. Who'd look after you then, huh?" He folded his burly arms over his stomach and smiled. "Have a good day."

Sadyra held his stare for as long as she dared. Scooping up the coins, she pushed through the door, unable to keep herself from muttering under her breath, "Low down, dirty rotten, ill-begotten lump of—"

"Sadyra!" Swab called to her from the middle of her boat, a bailer in hand. "I got most of the water out for you."

She glared at him, barely catching the irate retort that had found its way into the forefront of her mind. If her father hadn't worn out his welcome with every fishery from here to Madrigail Bay, she would never do business with the likes of the North Shore Fishery. That being said, Swab didn't deserve her wrath. Thinking about it, the boy was one of the kindest people she knew. He always had a smile for her.

She faked a smile for his sake. "Thank you, Swab. That's very kind of you."

Swab looked away, his cheeks reddening. "Aw, shucks, Sadyra. You say the nicest things. You know I would do anything for you."

As foul a mood as Skipper had put her in, Swab's genuine sincerity whisked it aside. A heartfelt grin replaced her fake smile. "I know, and I appreciate it."

She held out a hand to help him onto the dock.

"Thank you." Swab smiled from ear to ear as he stood beside her, not releasing her hand.

"Um…"

Swab followed her gaze to their hands. He released her and looked at his feet. "Oh! I'm sorry. I-I…"

"Don't sweat it," Sadyra said as she jumped in behind the bench and waited for Swab to untie the boat.

Swab deftly released the bow line first and tossed it to her.

She watched him do the same with the aft rope. Accepting the coil, she stowed it beneath the stern outwale and fought the surf with her oars to keep from being dashed against the pier.

Swab appeared poised to jump to her rescue should she lose control of the craft.

She waited for a wave to roll by and oared the bow around to face the ocean. As she plied the oars, she felt uncomfortable under Swab's scrutiny. To break the awkwardness, she said, "A real shame about the fish market."

Swab nodded. "I'd say. If fish become any scarcer, you'll be fetching a king's ransom for your troubles."

Swab's genuine grin left her dumbfounded. Her oars stopped in mid row. "Huh?"

He ran to the end of the jetty and shouted to be heard over the crashing surf. "Aye! Perhaps tomorrow you'll have enough to open up your own fishery!"

Sadyra's face dropped. Feeling the pittance of coins in her pocket that Skipper had paid out, the dark rage her father had roused in her last night returned.

With clenched teeth, she drove the oars into the waves and pulled hard. A colder than usual breeze ruffled her hair across her face.

"Be careful out there!"

Sadyra gazed at Swab from beneath hardened brows.

Swab pointed toward the darkening western horizon. "A big storm's coming in!"

The village of Fishmonger Bay appeared much sooner than it normally would have. Fueled by a burning anger and the drift of the strong current, the coastal area she knew so well drew her attention. Swirling ocean swells broke ominously upon hidden shoals. The sky had darkened considerably as she made her way across the waves but luckily the storm had held off.

There was a wide break straight out from the village's lone pier, but keeping a boat floating straight in heavy seas driven by the approaching front, and avoiding the razor ridge reef, wasn't an easy thing to do.

Though not burdened by fish, the water Sadyra's boat had taken on during her return trip up the coast had its outwales riding low in the water. If she hadn't had to keep her total concentration on the oars, she might have been able to keep the boat relatively dry, but as it was, water sloshed around her shins. Her father's handyman skills left much to be desired.

Lining up the channel through the reef, Sadyra plied the oars—fighting to keep the rushing wave caps from breaching her boat.

Sadyra

Carried on a high swell, the little boat sped toward the shoreline. Rowing hard, she prevented the craft from drifting too much on the current.

As expected, everything happened quickly. Slipping into the trough behind the last wave, she steadied the boat's course and felt the tiny craft lifting on the next wave. With any luck, this one would carry her through the gap—leaving her rowing furiously to avoid being sucked back out and into the reefs.

The boat rose quickly, its speed picking up. Scary as it was, Sadyra was used to fighting the sea. Buoyed by the approaching storm, the wave's push was more violent than normal, but she didn't panic. No two waves were ever the same.

It wasn't until she noticed the curly froth forming that she realized she was in trouble. The great waves generally didn't break until closer to the reef, but the wave lifting her boat curled sooner than anticipated.

Looking up in horror, her little craft rose almost vertical. She searched for a safe place to dive into the surf, but couldn't see anything but razor-sharp rock exposed by the undertow of the building wave. The wave frothed overhead and thundered down, collapsing on top of her—capsizing the boat and throwing her head over heels into the pummeling surf.

Caught in the wave's clutches, she was helpless to do anything but hold her breath and pray. She anticipated the boat smashing into her or the bite of the unforgiving shoals as they ripped her to shreds but neither happened.

Thrown against the ocean floor, the side of her face and left shoulder hit hard. The undertow dragged her backward, preventing her from breaking free and swimming to the surface. The bulk of the wave passed overhead, but she was being sucked into the beginning of the next one.

She panicked, not knowing which way was up or down, or whether her efforts were taking her farther from shore.

Sadyra

Her lungs ached, threatening to burst. Breaking through the surface of the front of the next wave she jerked her head out of the way to avoid being hit by her upside-down boat.

The pull of the building wave dragged her upward. She snatched a quick look at her surroundings. The village lay beyond the wall of jagged rock exposed in the trough in front of the wave she rode.

The vision of her irate father dominated her thoughts. If she allowed the boat to get damaged again, he would flay her unconscious. Growing up on the ocean, she put her proficient swimming skills to the test and tried to reach the boat with the hope of guiding it through the visible gap on her right.

The building wave drew her and the boat north of the opening toward the worst of the reef. She hazarded a glance over her shoulder and her breath caught. The wave was cresting. Once it broke, she would lose control of herself and the boat.

Three quick strokes brought her alongside the overturned craft, but as she pushed on its sides, her grasping fingers slid off its slippery hull. Kicking hard and flailing her arms in a desperate effort to catch the boat, she was aware of a thunderous roar overhead.

The wave fell on her, driving her under and spinning her out of control. The force of the wave slammed her against the ocean floor, driving the air from her lungs.

She sucked in a mouthful of seawater and started to cough—a painful rush entered her lungs. She broke through the surface, coughing violently and spewing salty brine.

A sickening crack sounded nearby. Her boat broke against the reef as her body bumped against the edge of the channel and drifted toward shore.

A gentler undertow tried to drag her back out to sea but she jammed her boots into the rocky ocean floor and held her position.

Sadyra

Another wave rose up beyond the reef. Caught in its pull were two large pieces of her boat. They climbed slowly higher, drifting northward on the rising wall until the wave broke upon the reef, showering the turbulent water beyond with mist, foam, and splinters of the Ors' family boat.

Incredulous, Sadyra watched her life disintegrate before her eyes, for as the fortunes of the boat went, so did her own. She had given her father ample reason to beat her senseless.

A momentary urge to let herself be whisked out to sea with the next surge washed through her. If not for her sisters' welfare—Sable's in particular—she might have.

Distant voices reached her. Villagers called out, but she paid them no mind. She couldn't concentrate on anything other than the despairing notion of her father's imminent reaction.

As the aftermath of the next wave washed over her, lifting her from the ocean bottom and carrying her toward shore, she half expected to see her father waiting there. The water reversed direction and it was all she could do to anchor herself and resist its tow.

"Sadie!" A set of strong hands wrapped themselves under her arms and around her chest, pulling her toward the shore. Vaguely aware of Bano's voice, she didn't care. As much as she wanted to be strong for Sleena and Sable, she couldn't help slipping back into the mind frame of wanting to drown herself in the ocean to avoid the impending meeting with her father.

"Stop struggling! You'll drown us both!"

She had no idea what she was doing. Trying to clear her mind of jumbled thoughts, she became aware that her struggles were dragging her and Bano toward the channel.

She let herself go limp. Regardless of how she felt about Bano, this wasn't his fault. It didn't seem fair to be the cause of his death as well.

Sadyra

Gravel crunched beneath Bano's boots as he dragged her from the water and sat her down amongst a circle of concerned and curious villagers.

Dreamily, she searched their faces. Father Cloth and his wife were there; their lips moving in what she knew would be blessings, but their words didn't register. Boys and girls of all ages knelt or leaned in—everyone asking if she was okay, but she barely heard them. All that echoed in her mind was the sickening crack of the family boat as the waves churned it into driftwood; coupled with her father's angry words repeating themselves over and over, *'Next time you hit a reef, you best pray your head's between the boat and the rock.'*

Bano knelt before her, holding her cheeks in his palms and staring into her eyes. "Sadie. Are you okay?"

She nodded as everything became clear around her. She pulled out of his grasp and looked at the concerned faces watching her. Her cheeks reddened.

"We'd best get you out of here." Bano slipped in behind and slid his hands under her armpits, lifting her to her feet.

The ground lurched and reeled—her body still believing it was on the water.

Bano held her by the forearm and elbow, using a gentle but firm pressure to direct her away from the shoreline. He nodded and put on a smile for the villagers. "I've got her. She'll be fine. She's just a little shook up."

He leaned in close. "Come on. Your father was in the *Cauldron*. News will reach him quick."

She turned a groggy gaze at Bano and blinked several times. Her father? In the *Cauldron*? Her eyes grew wide at the thought.

"Aye. We need to hide you."

She swallowed and shook her head, trying to break free of his strong hands.

"What do you mean, no? He'll kill you."

"I have to get Sable and Sleena." She ran a hand over her sodden tunic and gaped in disbelief.

"What is it?"

"My money. I lost it. All of it." She ripped her arm free of his grasp and started for the buildings fronting the trailhead.

"Sadie, wait. You can't go home. If he catches you…"

His words were lost on her. Driven by an all consuming need to extricate her sisters from the impending storm, she only had thoughts of reaching her cabin and spiriting them away. The crushing sensation that the money was gone made her weak in the knees.

Bano's protests followed her up the hill but with every stride she outdistanced the stocky boy. She had always been a good runner. Living atop the steep hill overlooking Fishmonger Bay, travelling back and forth to the village had conditioned her legs for climbing.

Sprinting up the side path toward the cabin proper, she feared what her mother would say. The insufferable woman always knew when she was lying.

The door squealed and banged against the outside wall as she burst into the dimly lit hut. Sleena and Sable were inside. A great sigh of relief eased her mounting fear. Sleena and their mother mended clothes by the table while Sable sat in the small sleeping area the three sisters shared, playing with a cornstalk doll Sadyra had made for her the previous Mating Festival.

"What is it, child?" Areeza dropped her sewing into her lap. Eyes narrowed, she inspected Sadyra's wet clothing and dishevelled hair. "What have you done?"

Sadyra stared at her mother, not knowing what to say. She hoped Bano would be along shortly to take her mother's attention from her.

Her gaze darted about the room, falling on her bow and quiver propped against the wall. She'd have to pass her mother to get to them.

Sadyra

Areeza slammed her sewing on the table and stood to block Sadyra's advance.

Sadyra made to go around her but Areeza kicked a stool across her path, upending it, and pointed a finger in her face.

"I asked you a question young lady."

Sadyra locked eyes, repulsed by the sour odour of mead on her mother's breath. Staring into Areeza's hazel eyes, two things struck her. Sable shared their mother's eyes *and* Sadyra wasn't a child anymore.

For the first time in her life, her mother didn't frighten her. The woman was nothing but a drunken, old woman who, if she kept up this lifestyle, would have one foot in the grave with the other following quickly after in the very near future.

"Well?"

Spittle hit Sadyra's cheek. Disgusted, she slapped her mother's hand away and pushed past the teetering woman.

Areeza stumbled and arrested her fall by grabbing the table. Righting herself, she scrambled to intercept Sadyra.

Sadyra spun and raised her own finger—her storm-grey eyes full of fury. "Don't!"

"You little bi—" Areeza tried to slap Sadyra's face, but Sadyra's hand was quicker.

Catching her mother's wrist in an iron grip, she twisted it outward and down, forcing her mother to her knees. Tears streamed down her cheeks as she regarded the sad excuse of a person who called herself their mom. Unable to keep her voice from cracking, Sadyra bent over her. "You ever touch us again, you'll be sorry. You hear?"

Sleena watched on, terror lighting her eyes.

Areeza struggled to free herself but Sadyra wrenched harder, causing her to yelp in pain.

"You hear me?"

Areeza growled through gritted teeth, "Wait 'til Tural finds out what you've done. He'll skin you alive."

Sadyra twisted and drove downward, forcing Areeza to cry out and roll on the floor. Releasing her, she rushed to Sable cowering in the corner, clutching her doll. "Come on. I'm taking you away from here." She glanced at Sleena. "You too. Grab what's important and let's go."

Areeza shakily got to her knees by hanging onto the upturned stool. "What do you think you're doing?"

Sadyra collected her bow, quiver, and the special clothes she like to wear while hunting. Grabbing Sable's wrist, she yanked the young child to her feet harder than she meant to.

Areeza fell back against the counter. She reached behind her and produced a long knife used to carve meat. Malice contorting her features, she advanced on Sadyra. "You're not taking them anywhere."

Sleena screamed and Sable squealed but Sadyra met their mother with her filleting knife in hand.

Areeza's hand trembled visibly; her gaze focused on Sadyra's knife. "You wouldn't dare."

Sadyra released Sable and lunged—a wild swing barely missing Areeza's face. She didn't recognize her own voice. "Try me."

Watching her mother drop the knife and stumble against the counter, Sadyra was unable to control the adrenaline surging through her. "That was a warning. Threaten me again and make no mistake, I *will* kill you."

Sadyra turned to Sleena. "You got what you need?"

Sleena appeared too terrified to speak. Hands empty, she nodded.

"Good." Not taking her eyes off Areeza, Sadyra knelt in front of Sable. "Come on, sweetie. We have to go."

Sable's timid eyes stared at Sadyra above the head of her doll. "You're scaring me, Sadie."

Guilt trembled Sadyra's lower lip, but she knew what she had to do. "It's okay. You never have to be scared again as long as I'm around." She shouldered her bow and quiver, and forced a smile for Sable's sake. "Do you love me?"

Sable nodded ever so slightly.

"And I love you. I won't allow anything bad to happen to you. Okay?"

Sable's eyes darted from Sadyra to Sleena to their mother and back. She nodded.

"Give me your hand."

Sable didn't appear as if she heard, but eventually she grabbed onto Sadyra.

"That's it. Sadie's got you." Sadyra sheathed her knife and held out her other hand for Sleena. "Come on. You too. We're sisters."

Sleena's eyes never left their scowling mother but she accepted Sadyra's hand with a strong grip.

Areeza's voice followed them out of the cabin. "Just you wait! All of you! Your father will teach you a lesson you won't soon forget!"

Not bothering to close the door, Sadyra marched her sisters to the junction with the main path and looked down the trail toward the village. Her anger spent; her earlier bravado left her wanting a plan of action. Now that she had rescued Sleena and Sable, she didn't know what to do. Absently, she wondered what had happened to Bano.

The Summoning Stone lay cold and bare to the north. Beyond that point there was nothing but rugged mountainside all the way to a great valley known as Dragonfang Pass. She had once travelled to a peculiar jag of granite her father had called the Fang. He said it marked the western entrance to Dragonfang Pass, and that all who went there never came back.

Knowing her father as she did now, she didn't trust most things he had told her over the years. Floundering under the influence of alcohol and harbouring some dark secret, his words were more likely meant to deceive than educate.

As far as she knew, nobody lived north of their cabin. She momentarily considered fleeing into the wilds. If not for her sisters, she would have, but their welfare was paramount. She dreaded the consequences of a rash decision.

Conscious of the fact that Sleena and Sable watched her, she swallowed and wiped away tears. She must be strong for their sake.

For no discernable reason, Swab came to mind. The kindly fishmonger would help her, surely.

Fishmonger Bay lay at the bottom of the steep hill. All she had to do was get past the village and head down the coastal road toward Thunderhead.

She shivered. Nobody travelled that way lightly. The ever-present danger of trolls forced most people to sail to the port city. Looking to the brooding sky, the afternoon sun lay hidden somewhere over the Niad Ocean. She wasn't sure how long it took to travel the coastal route, but she was certain they'd never make Thunderhead before nightfall. Being caught on the mountain after dark was not something she cared to entertain.

Bano! That was it. They could hide at Bano's until morning. He would do anything for her. If the storm had passed by then, she would set out at first light and take her sisters away from here.

"Sadie, I'm scared."

Sable's meek voice brought another wave of tears to Sadyra's eyes. Biting her lower lip, she thought, *So am I.*

Sadyra hardened her stare. She didn't have time to be scared. It was her fault they were in this position.

Lifting Sable into the crook of one arm she held out a hand for Sleena. "Come on. I won't let Father *or* Mother hurt you anymore."

Of the three of them, Sleena looked the least like the other two. Her fair hair and green eyes bespoke of different parentage. Sadyra had always thought Sleena was different, but until this moment, she had never thought they might not share the same parents. If anything, Sleena resembled their father.

The sound of a door slamming directed Sleena's attention up the path.

Sadyra

Sadyra feared their mother had followed them, but no one appeared. Her eyes flicked to the half-hidden gravestones and found herself wishing that she knew what secrets their owners contained.

Wiggling her fingers, she prompted Sleena's cold hand to grab hers and smiled for her benefit. "We'll be okay. You'll see."

They walked a few steps down the path when Sadyra froze. Yanking Sleena into the heather, she knelt with Sable on her thigh. It took her a moment to realize that the man lying prone across the pathway wasn't their father. It was Bano.

Sadyra put Sable down and had her join hands with Sleena. "Stay here."

At first, she thought he was dead, but Bano's subtle chest falls told her otherwise. A trickle of blood at the corner of his lip and a nasty bruise beside his eye gave evidence that he had been in a fight. With a sinking feeling, she knew with who.

A quick scan of the immediate area proved fruitless. The tops of her sisters' heads could be seen in the underbrush beside the trail but no one else was in sight.

"Bano. Speak to me." Sadyra knelt and shook his shoulders but got no response. She grabbed his cheeks much like he had held hers on the beach. "Bano. It's me. Sadie."

At the mention of her nickname, Bano groaned. His head rolled in her hands and his eyes opened with a pain-laced squint. He struggled to focus but as his gaze locked on hers, he sat upright and looked around.

Startled, Sadyra fell onto her backside. "It's okay. It's me."

"Sadie?" Bano stood and scanned the hillside, his attention falling on Sleena and Sable. "Where's your father?"

Sadyra got to her feet—dirt and grass sticking to her damp clothing. "I don't know. I haven't seen him."

"You have to run. I tried to intercept him but he hit me and cut across the hill toward your cabin."

Sadyra followed his gaze, noticing for the first time the faint trace of trampled foliage angling away from the path toward where their cabin lay; hidden by trees and underbrush.

Movement at the top of the hill chilled Sadyra to the bone.

Tural Ors looked down at them, his chest heaving above the axe in his hands.

Sadyra

Wrecked

Tural Ors roared something indecipherable, but Sadyra knew it was aimed at her as the boor of a man strode with purpose down the path.

She searched for an escape route, fingering her knife. Her gaze locked on her sisters' frightened faces. There was no way she could outdistance their father with Sleena and Sable at her side.

She thought of her bow, but doubted she could string it quick enough to get an arrow off.

Bano strode past her to confront Tural.

"Bano, no!" Sadyra grabbed him by the shoulder and spun him around. Speaking as quietly as her panic allowed, she said, "Take my sisters to someplace safe until I return."

Bano frowned.

"Just do it." She shrugged free of her quiver and handed it and her bow to Bano; shoving him toward Sleena and Sable. Her sisters backed away from the trail and the approach of their father. "Now!"

Bano scrambled to the young girls and ushered them deeper into the underbrush.

Sadyra feared her father might go after them but knew in her heart that he would ignore them. His anger was directed at her.

Tural took a couple of steps off the trail and raised his tree-chopping axe after Bano and her sisters but staggered back onto the beaten path. He adjusted his grip on the axe; an evil grin lifting his unshaven cheeks. "I should've done this the day you were born."

Certain her legs were about to buckle, Sadyra stumbled backward. Her gaze flicked to where her sisters and Bano had disappeared behind a copse of trees.

Following her gaze, Tural snarled, "I'll deal with them later. It's time your mother and I were rid of our burden."

Sadyra waggled her knife, amazed she had the nerve to stand up to him.

Tural's features darkened. "What're you gonna do with that? Trim my nails?" A maniacal laugh escaped his throat. He slapped the handle of the axe in an upturned palm. "Perhaps I'll use it to skin the sorry hide of a nettlesome witch."

Sadyra's outstretched hand trembled violently as his words echoed in her mind, *'...skin the sorry hide of a nettlesome witch...skin the sorry hide of a nettlesome witch...'*

Tural raised his axe.

Driven by terror, Sadyra grabbed a rock and threw it at him. The clumsily thrown stone clattered harmlessly against Tural's forearm, but the action was enough to break the paralysis his presence had on her. Stepping back, she spun and sprinted down the hill.

The clang of Tural's axe bouncing off the ground at her heels made Sadyra jump and squeal. Hazarding a glance over her shoulder, her father crashed into the heather to retrieve it—allowing her to put more distance between them.

Running hard, she stumbled and fell, barely hanging onto her knife as the steep trail levelled out and passed between two buildings. She was only on the ground for a moment before rolling to her feet. Steadying herself on the back corner of a building, she watched her father charging recklessly down the hill. As drunk and old as he was, his dogged determination filled her with dread. He wouldn't give up until he had vented his wrath.

Several townspeople stopped what they were doing to watch her sprint across the commons and disappear around the steps fronting the village temple.

Sadyra thought about banging on Father Cloth's door but decided against it. Her father would go right through the man to get to her. She didn't want to be the cause of the holy man's demise.

She pulled up on the far side of the temple and stared at the *Witch's Cauldron* nestled against the base of the towering cliff hemming in the village. Something about the tavern made her skin crawl. Everything Bano had relayed to her over the past months filled her with an eerie, prickling sensation. The gravestones on the hill. Her family home, and the rumours of the people who had once lived there. Bano's talk of the Dragon Witch being her distant relative.

Folklore claimed the *Witch's Cauldron* was named after a notorious village witch who had once owned a different building on that very spot, centuries ago. If she believed the tales, the villagers of the time had rid themselves of the witch by locking her in it and burning the hut to the ground.

Her rapid chest falls—more fear than exertion—made it hard to listen for Tural's approach. Peering around the corner, she rose to the tip of her toes but couldn't see him. With a sinking feeling, she glanced at the rear corner of the temple.

Her father stepped out from behind the building.

Sadyra rounded the front of the temple and mounted the long flight of steps two at a time. Before she could try the door, the steps shook as Tural burst around the corner and latched onto the railing to help him change direction.

Lightning flashed over the ocean—a deep crack of thunder rumbling on its heels

"I've got you now."

Sadyra grabbed the long handles of the double doors and pulled. Fearing they were locked, they opened with a loud squeal.

Sadyra

The interior of the temple lay bathed in shadow. Soft light filtered through high windows, illuminating rows of benches lining either side of a narrow aisle that led to two wide steps fronting a small altar.

Sadyra sprinted up the aisle, her eyes searching for an escape route. She had been in the temple many times before, but only once had she seen beyond the apse. Vaulting the altar steps in a single bound, she heard the doors slam against the outside railing.

“Don’t be looking to Father Cloth to save you. You’re my whelp to do with as I please.”

She didn’t look back. Three quick steps took her to a hidden alcove at the rear of the apse. A narrow hallway curved around the back of the altar and stopped at a single door.

Sadyra grasped its small handle and gasped. It was locked.

Her father’s footsteps pounded onto the altar, sounding through the wall as if he were right on top of her.

Jiggling the handle, Sadyra pushed at the door with her shoulder. The thin wooden panel gave a little but the latch held fast.

Hurried footfalls crossed the apse toward the far end of the hallway—the floorboards squeaking in protest.

Sadyra stared down the dark hallway. Her father would be on her in no time. She swallowed heavily, stepped back, and kicked at the door repeatedly; grunting with frustration each time.

The far end of the hallway darkened as Tural charged toward her.

One last everything or nothing kick cracked the door panel. She threw her shoulder against it and fell to her side as it gave way. Not waiting to see where her father was, she scrambled onto her hands and knees and gained her feet. Several strides took her to the top of a flight of steps leading into darkness below.

Sadyra

She half-stepped, half-stumbled down the worn wooden flight—jarring herself when she reached the ground.

Wherever she had ended up was devoid of light. Using her hands to feel along the walls, she bashed her shins and feet repeatedly off unseen obstructions. She feared the room didn't have an exit, but it wasn't long before she felt the frame of a doorway. Locating the handle, it gave way beneath her touch, pulling into the room and emitting a meagre light from a lone window on the opposite wall. She slammed the door behind her

The sound of Tural's hurried tumble down the stairs got her feet moving toward a door beside the window. She cried out in dismay as she pushed down and lifted its handle. It wouldn't open.

Her gaze took in the dim interior, searching for another exit. Dark shapes lined the walls, but she couldn't see much behind them. Beside her, an old stool sat against the wall beneath the window; butted against a wooden chair with a broken leg.

The rear door ripped open. Tural's silhouette filled the doorway. "Stop running, witch. It's time you met your ancestors."

Sadyra didn't think twice. She grabbed the broken chair and smashed the window—the chair breaking in her hands. Dropping one piece, she hurled another across the room.

Tural dodged out of the way, but his momentary distraction allowed her to mount the wobbly stool and dive through the window.

Her thigh caught on a shard of glass still in the sill. Landing in a heap at the rear of the temple, she didn't have time to worry about the searing pain in her leg.

A rain drop splattered against her cheek.

She looked first to the *Witch's Cauldron* and then the other way at the rear of the mercantile built against the base of the unscalable cliff.

Tural slammed into the door—the thick wood groaning but not giving way. His angry face appeared at the window. Using the axe head, he brushed at the remaining shards lining the sill and started to climb through. His deranged eyes found hers. "You evil witch. You're making this worse for yourself."

Sadyra jumped to her feet and ran around the corner between the mercantile and the temple. She considered fleeing back up the hill, but the sight of a couple people standing near the buildings fronting the trail head made her change her course. Instead, she ran across the gravelly commons toward the long building housing Fishmonger Bay's only real fishery; all the while wishing she hadn't given her bow to Bano.

At least her sisters were safe. As long as she remained alive, Tural wouldn't turn his attention their way.

She hoped to slip beyond the fishery and out of sight before he spotted her, but as she rounded the far corner of the building, Tural appeared around the front corner of the temple.

For the briefest of moments, she entertained seeking refuge within the fishery, but thought better of it. Inside she would likely find herself surrounded by hardened sailors who wouldn't take kindly to being disturbed. These men were as tough as Tural. She had visited the building many times with her father but she wasn't sure it was wise to try her luck without him.

Halfway along the warehouse wall facing the oceanside, she froze, cursing herself. She didn't know which side of the building Tural would come around, nor could she risk returning the way she had come.

A stabbing pain throbbed above her left knee. Her deerskin leggings were torn open—the gaping material stained red with blood. The glass shard from the temple window had gashed her worse than she thought.

Sadyra

A violent thunder crack echoed off the mountainside. The skies opened up, drenching her instantly.

She staggered backward across the beach toward the jetty, her squinted eyes watching both corners of the building. Movement from the far corner caused her feet to move back the way she had come, but it wasn't her father. She had no sooner taken two steps than Tural rounded the same corner she had.

Her father's eyes fell on her and then spotted the sailor at the far end of the building. Through the downpour, she couldn't hear what he said, but the sailor yelled something back and disappeared into the warehouse.

Tural walked toward her in no apparent hurry.

Jumping into a run, Sadyra took three quick steps toward where the sailor had disappeared and stopped as the warehouse door opened.

The original sailor exited and pointed her way as two others followed. Oblivious to the teeming rain, they pushed their short sleeves up their muscled arms and started her way; fanning out to keep her from escaping along the shoreline.

She thought about trying to slip past her father but Tural advanced midway between the warehouse and the water. She doubted she stood a chance of avoiding the reach of his axe.

The only route left to her was the angry surf at her back. A quick glance showed her that the waves smashing the reef lining the mouth of the small bay hadn't diminished since she capsized. If anything, they had grown in size, pushed on by the cusp of the storm. A series of lightning bolts jagged over the waves, illuminating a two-masted boat listing in the face of the wind. The brig could only be Fishmonger Bay's chief fishing boat, the *Catch*, caught out in the storm.

Sadyra sprinted along the slippery planks lining the pier—bracing herself as a large wave formed inside the reef and slammed into it.

The original sailor reached the end to the dock first; his voice barely audible over the heavy surf and relentless downpour. "Stop! You'll be swept out to sea!"

Sadyra wanted to laugh. How was that worse than being hacked to death by her father?

The other sailors joined their mate but they didn't move onto the jetty. They gave Tural a wide berth as he caught up to them. The original sailor tried to talk Tural out of chasing her into the dangerous conditions but her father ignored him.

Tural's methodical footfalls followed her out over the water. The remains of a crashing wave washed over the top of his boots, breaking on his thighs and splashing into his face. He continued as if it hadn't happened.

Left with no choice, Sadyra prepared to dive into the surf.

Lightning flashed and a thunderclap rattled off the cliff face towering over the village.

Illuminated by the storm, the fishing brig rose high on a wave, its bow pointed at the narrow channel between the reefs.

Sadyra shuddered—her recent attempt at the channel fresh in her mind. Whoever was captaining that ship was as insane as she had been for attempting to enter the bay.

"Looks like you injured yourself," Tural snarled. He must have understood what she was thinking. "You've got nowhere left to run, but go ahead and do it. Let's see if witches really do float." He snickered. "You'll not survive the sea a second time. I promise you that."

Sadyra bent her knees to jump, ignoring the pain. Fear of being dashed into the dock as another wave crested and broke over the seaward end of the pier stopped her. Battered by the force of the wave, she dropped to her hands and knees to keep from being washed over the side. If not for the broken planks she latched onto, she would have.

Tural leaned into the remnants of the wash, its force staggering him backward, but on he came.

"Father! It was an accident!"

"Aye, witch. You most certainly are."

His words robbed her of what she wanted to say next. Gaping, she felt sorry for the drunken man who carried a dark secret. Sorry for the man who was supposed to be her father—someone who was supposed to love and protect her no matter what. He had never been anything of the sort.

Her parents blamed her for something she hadn't done. Some curse they claimed she had brought on with her birth, but they never spoke openly of it.

In her heart, she knew her father's present rage stemmed from the burden of that curse. Though the destruction of the family boat had been the catalyst of his rampage, his loathing of her went much deeper. Facing an imminent brush with death, she wished, not for the first time, that her parents would have had the courtesy to let her know what it was that lay at the root of their discontent.

Her mind snapped back to the present. A few more steps and he would be within reach. She had no doubt he would slay her.

She considered the knife in her hand. There was no way.

She sheathed the blade and eyed an approaching wave; diving into its body to avoid the violent crest that broke over the pier and lifted Tural from his feet; slamming him onto the dock several steps back.

The cold water took her breath away. Weighed down by her clothing and boots, she struggled to break through the surface. Gasping for air, it took a moment to regain her bearings. The surging currents of the swells pulled her away from the dock and farther out to sea.

Catching sight of the shoreline through the relentless downpour, she followed it to the jetty. Joined by the other sailors, one of them pointing in her direction, her father screamed something unintelligible and shook his fist but it was lost to the roar of the surf.

Tural leaned back and pitched forward; his axe twirling through the air in a great arc. Handle over axe head, Sadyra was powerless to move as the next wave pulled her toward the channel. Flinching, she ducked beneath the water.

The axe missed her by the slightest of margins and sunk.

Caught in the undertow, she held her breath and desperately tried to remove her boots. Filled with water, they wouldn't budge.

Her earlier escapade in the surf left her determined not to relive the awful sensation of breathing seawater. Touching down on the ocean floor, she bent her knees and pushed hard; breaking the surface with a wracking cough.

Panic set in. The shoreline was farther away. Hidden by the roiling waves and with more pressing issues to deal with, she didn't worry whether she could see the jetty and her father any longer.

Barely able to keep her head above water, she flailed her arms and legs, turning to face the reef.

The *Catch* had poised itself to enter the channel on the next wave. From where Sadyra floundered, the channel opening lay exposed. Given the strength of the tidal pull, she knew at once the brig had drifted too far.

The water lifted her. Not waiting for the crest, she ducked into the swell and fought to swim out of its backside. Years of swimming in the strong currents of the Niad Ocean had conditioned her to its nuances but her muscles screamed.

Breaking through the surface, she watched in horror. The *Catch* rose on a large wave, drifting beyond the channel. The wave frothed and broke, collapsing over the stern and broaching the craft. The *Catch* rolled sideways. Its masts slapped the bottom of the wave and snapped.

Sadyra cringed. A tell-tale crack of wood rose above the chaos as the wave smashed against the unforgiving ridge. Cries of despair hauntingly serenaded the mangled sections of timber and sailcloth churning within the breaking water.

The aftermath of the killing wave washed over her in a rush of splintered debris. Taking advantage of the landward push, she swam as fast as her beleaguered limbs would carry her.

Sadyra

The shoreline beckoned, but her momentum died on the ocean floor as an ominous lull heralded the inevitable undertow. Try as she might, in water over her head, she couldn't escape its grip.

Frantic shouts of sailors who had somehow survived the wreck surrounded her, but she couldn't see anyone in the tossing waves. In a desperate struggle to keep her head above water, only black clouds roiling overhead and the surging sea littered with barrels, broken yard arms, and sections of shattered hull were visible.

A large wave broke on the reef sending a powerful surge of water and man-sized splinters tumbling toward her. Grasping the ends of a barrel, she ducked behind it to prevent the wreckage from tearing into her. The swell caught hold of the barrel; collecting it and her into its maelstrom.

Something snagged at her flailing boots, threatening to drag her under. The barrel slipped from her hands. Catching one last glimpse of the jetty, the old dock defied the storm; its deck devoid of people.

Sinking beneath the waves with no way to untangle herself from a fishnet that had wrapped her legs in a cocoon, an odd sense of relief eased her terror. Her father wouldn't catch her.

Prepared to succumb to her fate, her eyes blinked open. If she died, her father would turn his unspent rage on Sable and Sleena.

The more she squirmed, the tighter the netting became. Dragging along the ocean floor, she couldn't believe her life was ending this way.

Sadyra

"Salvage everything you can," A deep voice resonated in Sadyra's foggy consciousness. "Pile the bodies and the wreckage over there. We'll burn them in the morn."

Not caring for the sound of that, she had bigger things to worry about. Her mouth tasted of sea water and vomit, and her eyes were crusted shut. She tried to wipe at her eyelids but her arms wouldn't move. They were wrapped around her abdomen at uncomfortable angles, bound tight by a…a fishing net!

The last thing she remembered before stirring at the sound of the man's voice was sinking to the ocean floor—pulled under by the weight of a massive net. An underwater surge had grabbed hold of her and the net and slammed them against something hard. A white light had flashed in her head and now she was here.

"What about the net?" A voice from farther away asked.

A strong gust of wind sent shivers through her. She absently noted the rain had stopped.

The first voice sounded below her.

"As long as it hasn't suffered too much damage, we might be able to save it from the fire."

Sadyra gulped. She couldn't imagine the men not being able to see her entangled in the net, but if they hadn't and it was deemed the net wasn't salvageable…

She almost cried out to let them know she was in the net but thought better of it. She had no idea where her father had gotten to. If he was around and caught her like this, she would be helpless to protect herself. A cold dread gripped her. If he *wasn't* here, he'd be searching out Bano and her sisters.

Tears of frustration and fear squeezed from the corners of her eyes—loosening the grit holding her eyelids shut. Through blurred vision she saw that she lay tangled in a knot of rope and debris, suspended several feet off the ground by a davit that had been erected on the edge of the gravel shoreline. Above, low lying clouds swirled beneath a higher layer covering the sky.

She squirmed her shoulders back and forth to loosen the hold the net had on her but it was no use. Her shoulders were sore and her arms numb. She tried wiggling her fingers and was shocked to find she couldn't feel them.

Something bumped the net from the far side, making it sway back and forth. The deep voice startled her, "There's a few cuts on this side but I think we can save it. Swing it over by the pyre and remove that shit."

Footsteps crunched below but she couldn't turn her head to see who it was.

"You believe that lunatic?" The second voice she'd heard asked.

"Pfft. He's always been a few fins short of a fish," replied a new voice.

"What's he thinking?"

"Dunno, but if he shows his face around here again, we're gonna have words."

"Ye'd best watch your back with that one. He's not right in the head."

"Don't scare me. If he tries anything, I'll shove his head up his arse."

"Ha! I'd like to see that."

The male voices faded as the men walked around the backside of the net.

Sadyra swallowed and struggled harder. If she wasn't mistaken, she could tell that the fingers on her lower hand moved. Flexing her back and shoulder muscles, she shrugged and attempted to turn her hand.

A warm sensation coursed down her arm and painfully rooted in her fingers; tingling with renewed blood flow.

The net jerked.

"Wait! Let me guide it from the other side. Don't want to damage the figurehead," The deep voice ordered. "Been in the family for centuries."

Sadyra frowned and searched the contents of the net that were visible to her limited line of sight. Barrels and deck planks were bound up all around her along with the odd dead fish and other things she couldn't readily identify, but as the net swayed inland, a golden figurehead the size of her family's old boat creaked higher up in the tangled mess, threatening to tip the load. If they lowered the net, the intricately carved dragon with wings furled by its side, and holding a large fish in front of its gaping mouth, appeared like it was poised to crush her.

Eyes focused on the row of fangs lining the figurehead's mouth, Sadyra struggled harder. The back of her hand burned as the rope chafed her skin, but she didn't have time to worry about the pain. She had to escape.

She feared she might dislocate her shoulder as she contorted her arm around the debris pinned against her. Locating her filleting knife, she bit her lips to stifle the pain of twisting her wrist to slide the knife free and began slicing at what she hoped was netting.

The knife's keen edge bit into the waterlogged rope. Had her father not been so anal about keeping her tools in top shape, she doubted the knife would have cut through the tough strands.

"Alright. Steady. Turn it slowly," the deep voice ordered and the net jerked away from the shoreline. An ominous creaking sounded from overhead.

In a state of panic, she almost dropped her knife as it broke through the first link. If her efforts had done anything useful, she couldn't tell. Craning her wrist at an uncomfortable angle, her blade found another strand.

The net swayed back and forth, precariously balanced on the end of the beach davit. It jerked forward and almost tipped.

Sadyra's wide eyes were locked on the figurehead teetering on whatever unstable mass lay beneath it.

"Whoa!" the deep voice cautioned. "Wreck my dragon and I'll wreck you!"

The net stopped moving.

Gravel crunched beneath her. Pressing her face against the mesh, she caught sight of a stocky, bald-headed man with an oft broke nose. She recognized him as the owner of the warehouse and the captain of the *Catch*, but couldn't remember if she had ever heard speak his real name. Everyone simply referred to him by his nautical title.

Wearing nothing but brown breeks and knee-high black leather boots, the captain knelt and studied the underside of the suspended bundle.

Despite her immediate danger, Sadyra couldn't help thinking he should wear a belt as the top of his hairy backside was exposed in his kneeling position. She looked away.

"Okay. Slower this time."

The second voice complained from where the davit operated. "If we go any slower, we'll be moving backward."

"If you give me anymore lip, *you'll* be moving backward. On the end of my fist! Now do it. Easy like."

The second voice grumbled something incoherent, but the net started to sway. Slowly, it rotated away from the water—the crash of the surf noticeably calmer than it had been during the storm.

A second length of rope broke beneath the pressure of her knife. Her body shifted slightly downward. Unfortunately, so did the wreckage around her.

She cast a worried glance at the figurehead but it hadn't moved.

Her hand and wrist dropped through the opening she made, allowing her room to manipulate her blade. Locating the next weave of net, her knife made quick work of it. One by one, she severed the tight mesh. As her knife cut through another length, her backside fell through.

She screeched in surprise—catching her exclamation in mid-voice, but the damage was done.

The captain backed out from beneath the bulging net and looked up. "There's a woman stuck in the netting!"

Fearing her father might be near, Sadyra sliced at the rope beside her injured thigh in a frenzied effort to allow the rest of her body to wriggle through.

"Hey! What're you doing? Stop cutting!" The captain commanded.

Sadyra's knife sawed quicker.

"Lower the net! Lower the net!" The captain ran toward where the davit had been erected, flailing his arms. Before he took three steps, he jumped back and shouted in dismay, "No!"

Sadyra's knife severed another link—instantly falling through the hole as the weight of the contents pushed her down. She hit the ground hard amid a shower of smaller debris, and rolled down the sloped beach.

A tumultuous clatter of entangled wreckage spewed through the hole and crashed to the ground. As the contents slid through the gap, they ripped the hole in the net wide open.

The sudden release of weight caused the davit to twist and topple sideways, barely missing two burly sailors. The net hit the ground with a resounding thump.

Sailors appeared from everywhere; running to see what all the commotion was about.

"My dragon!" The captain scrambled around the fallen net to where the figurehead lay half buried. His angry eyes found Sadyra crouched on the beach. "Grab her!"

Sadyra searched everywhere at once. Musclebound, no-nonsense men closed in around her. Not seeing her father did little to ease her apprehension. Picking a spot, she jumped to her feet and attempted to bolt between two of them.

One step on her injured leg dropped her to the stony ground in agony. Stiffness had made her leg react like a dead weight.

A pair of callused hands grabbed her arm and yanked her to her feet—the sailor's grip excruciating.

The captain walked up to her, glaring. "You're Tural's child, aren't you?"

Sadyra struggled but couldn't break the sailor's grip. Her eyes flitted everywhere at once, expecting her father to appear.

"Aren't you?" The captain roared, his nose a hair's breadth from hers.

She swallowed. Not trusting her voice, she pulled her head back into the chest of the man holding her and nodded.

"Why does he want to hurt you? What've you done?"

She shook her head.

"Nothing? I find that hard to believe. No normal man goes after his daughter with an axe. You must've done something."

The man belonging to the second voice she had heard upon waking, cleared his throat and said through an unruly beard, "She's the one I was telling you about. Wrecked her boat on the reef around midday."

The captain nodded. "Ah. That explains it."

Sadyra gaped.

The captain held up his hands. "I'm not saying you deserve to be punished with an axe. No offense intended, but your father's a strange man. I can only imagine what he planned to do to you."

He sighed and stepped back, rubbing a palm over his bald head. His gaze fell on the figurehead and his face darkened. He pointed at the net. "If that figurehead's damaged, I'll deliver you to him myself."

Sadyra

Glaring at the man holding her, the captain ordered, "Take her inside until I see what damage has been done."

The captain's office inside the warehouse was cramped—its walls lined with shelves bearing charts and various tools that Sadyra had never seen before. On the far side of the table he used as a desk, a high-back wooden chair covered with discarded papers sat in front of a filthy window overlooking the warehouse floor.

She opened the door a crack but closed it again. The no-nonsense man who had half-dragged her into the office, leaned against a wall just outside. He gave her a stern look.

Thankful for the way the yellowed window obscured the curious stares directed her way from the workers on the other side of the glass, she sat on a wobbly stool and worried at the ugly gash above her knee.

Her breeks would require a lot of thread to close the tear, but she doubted she'd ever get the bloodstain from the deerskin. The raw, deep cut was littered with sand and small debris—crusted over with salt residue. She dreaded cleaning it whenever the captain allowed her to leave. *If* he allowed her to leave.

She sighed. Her mother would flay her for ruining a pair of breeks.

A door banged somewhere close by. Heavy footfalls stomped across floorboards. Even though she knew he was coming, she jumped when the door flew open and banged against the wall.

The captain filled the doorway, his unreadable angular face highlighted by a long, crooked nose. Intense, brown eyes bored into her. "If not for my considerable patience…"

The guard, looking over his shoulder, rolled his eyes.

"…and my sunny disposition, I would march you straight up that hill and deposit you in Tural's lap."

Relief flooded Sadyra. She dared not breathe lest he change his mind.

"My dragon miraculously suffered only minor damage in the wreck. Less than one might expect given the beating it took." He looked over his shoulder. "Must be dragon magic, eh, Scruff?"

"Aye. Whatever you say, Cap." The man referred to as Scruff, grunted and walked away.

The captain blinked after him. "Doubt it all you like. I tell ya, there's still dragon magic in these mountains. Mark my words. Someday, we'll see its return."

Scruff raised a dismissive hand, not bothering to turn around, and disappeared from Sadyra's view.

The captain pursed his lips, but said no more. Stepping into the office, he closed the door and squeezed past the edge of the desk to sit down. Not bothering to clear the papers, he lowered his backside but shot back up with a yelp.

The biggest cat Sadyra had ever seen screeched its displeasure and bolted from the chair, disappearing under the table. The shabby, grey-furred feline slammed into the closed door and darted underneath Sadyra's stool, growling and hissing.

The captain stormed around the desk and yanked the door open, nearly hitting Sadyra's knees with it. "Why you little, flea-bitten furball. Go catch mice like you're supposed to, you lazy, no good…"

The cat hissed and swiped at his probing boot. Its hind legs suddenly scrabbled to gain purchase on the dirty floorboards and bolted from the office with a loud mewl.

"Honestly." The captain shook his head and closed the door. Taking his seat, he slapped the tabletop and focused on Sadyra. "Now, where were we?"

Sadyra returned his gaze but said nothing.

"Ah, yes. We were deciding what to do with you."

Sadyra couldn't help scowling. She muttered, "*We* weren't doing anything. *You're* the one who feels the need to dictate what happens to me next."

Her words made him pause. He shook his head and said, "Seems we're alike, you and I."

Her face softened into a quizzical frown. She failed to see any similarities between the bald-headed brute and herself.

"Aye. We're captains of our own demise."

She frowned deeper, tilting her head to one side.

"We wrecked our boats." As he spoke, his rough features transformed into a look of comprehension. "And that's it, isn't it?"

Sadyra stared at him. She had no idea what he was going on about.

"Wrecking our boats on the reef. The loss of the *Catch* is certainly worth more in material possessions, but the loss of *your* leaky craft has exacted a graver toll. Tural seeks to punish you for the loss of his livelihood with your life, hmm?"

Sadyra swallowed, her eyes moistening. She couldn't hold his gaze.

"Aye. I thought so." The captain nodded and fell silent.

Though she didn't look up, she knew the captain watched her—could feel his gaze bore into her. As relieved as she was to be out of her father's path, she knew it was only temporary. Fear feathered up her spine. She needed to see to the safety of her sisters.

Mustering as much nerve as she could, she raised her gaze to meet his. "Can I go?"

The captain squinted. "Go? Where? I doubt Tural's anger has lessened. Knowing him, your escape will have heightened his displeasure. You're safe here until I decide what to do with you."

She gaped.

"Don't worry. He won't get two steps inside my building before my men stop him. I assure you that."

"B-but, why?"

It was the captain's turn to frown.

"Why would you want to help me? You don't even know me."

"Och. Sneera, I'm offended. I've known you since you were a wee lass. You're a hard one to forget."

"It's Sadyra."

"Why yes…" The captain coughed, covering his mouth. "I'm shocked you don't remember me."

Sadyra searched her memories. She certainly knew of the captain. Who didn't? Everybody knew everybody in Fishmonger Bay. But actually, *know* him? She didn't even know his real name. She shrugged.

"Anyway, I used to love how sassy and cheeky you were as a child. I remember more than once debating whether to smack you for your insolence or slap you on the back and commend you for the outlandish things that used to come out of your mouth." He paused, beaming at her. "Whatever happened to the old Sn—Sadyra?"

Taken aback, Sadyra didn't know what to say. He described her the way many people in the bay area thought of her. She'd been given a smacked bottom many times because of her inability to hold her tongue. How the captain knew her so well unnerved her.

Mulling it over, she could only put it down to the Mating Festival. Being one of the biggest stakeholders in the village, the captain would have presided over the organization and running of the event. As such, it made sense he would have had ample chance to observe her over the years. Where else but the Mating Festival were the eclectic people of Fishmonger Bay able to let go of their inhibitions for a time and allow their inner self to shine through?

"Well?" he prompted. "What happened to dampen your wild spirit? Don't worry. Whatever you say, won't leave these walls."

“Nothing.” She dropped her gaze to her lap, absently focusing on her injured thigh. “Just…” She hesitated, afraid to go on.

“Just what?” The captain leaned over his desk; sympathy evident in his voice. “Like I said. Ain’t no one gonna get you in here. You’ve seen my crew. They may be an obstinate bunch of hard asses, but I assure you, they’re loyal to me. If I say Tural isn’t allowed within these walls, which he isn’t, then Tural will not get within these walls. Okay?”

She nodded, but refused to meet his gaze. Wondering where to start, she began with her tale of the last festival when she had taken her sisters to the cabin at the summit of Peril’s Peak to save them from the fallout of her parents’ overzealous celebrations.

The captain sat back in his chair with folded arms, smiling and grimacing at the same time as she spoke of the details. He never once interrupted.

Speaking to the captain, it was as if the dam holding back her darkest fears had broken. Her memories of abuse, both physical and psychological, flowed from her lips as if the captain were her best friend. It felt awkward hearing herself expose her deepest secrets to someone she didn’t really know, but the fact that the captain was basically a stranger, for some reason, made the telling easier.

For as long as she could remember, her parents had harboured a grudge toward her. She never knew the happiness nor the bond she witnessed her friends experience with their parents. Her parents’ malaise, a term she equated with whatever lie at the root of their discontent, always seemed to ramp up with the approach of the Mating Festival. The closer the celebration, the poorer their attitudes became—especially toward her.

Curiously, once the festival passed, the angst and tension in the Ors’ household diminished to a dull ebb. As long as Sadyra did exactly as expected, life went on as usual. Do the chores, help Tural man the boat, keep her sisters out of harm's way as the day progressed and her mother and father sank further into their drinks. Everyday was the same, and yet, somehow, she learned how to move beyond the rigours placed upon her, and enjoy the brief periods of time she could snatch for herself to play and hang out with the other children of the village.

Up until that fateful day she had taken her sisters to the summit. From that point onward, Tural had seen to it that she was kept busy every waking hour. Still, Sadyra managed to eke time for herself. Once her parents had passed out for the evening, and before they woke the next morning, she kept herself busy planning for the day she would leave it all behind.

The noise in the warehouse had died off significantly by the time Sadyra determined she had said too much.

Gazing at the captain as if seeing him for the first time, she forced a meek smile.

The captain had tipped his chair to lean against the window. He observed her with his chin in hand. "I must confess, if half of what you say is true, I find myself feeling sorry for you."

Sadyra poised herself to adamantly defend that what she said was true, but the captain spoke first.

"Save it. It's your word against Tural's."

"What about my sisters? They can confirm everything I've said…Well most. The stuff they know about."

"Do you think they'd speak up?"

Sadyra swallowed. Her spirit sank. She lowered her gaze with a slight shake of her head.

"And that's the rub. Not to mention the fact they're your parents. The community has little jurisdiction over someone's children. Your parents are your lawful guardians. As such, they're obliged to mete out whatever punishment they deem fit."

He let his chair fall forward. "That being said, you've confirmed what most of us already know…" He paused as

Sadyra gaped. "Aye. Hard to hide much in a village this size."

He stood up and stretched. The warehouse floor lay dark except for a few sconces scattered along the walls. The sun had set sometime during Sadyra's tale. "Getting back to the fact that we both share a reckless trait when it comes to navigating boats."

Sadyra caught his smirk.

"If I'm not mistaken, you've wrecked yours more than once in the last couple of days."

She couldn't help the shy smile turning up her lips. "Hasn't been my finest hour."

"Ha! That's more like the girl I used to know. Now, what are we going to do about it?"

"We?"

"Aye, lass. Your family needs a new boat, and I'm out an expensive net."

Sadyra felt her cheeks redden.

"Seems to me that someone in this office is in need of a means to pay back her debt. Not only to me, but to her parents."

The faintest glimmer of hope seeped into her.

"Seeing that my main ship has been destroyed, I'll be needing more hands to replace the daily catch. From what I've observed over the last few years, you've become quite a proficient fisherman."

"Woman," Sadyra muttered under her breath.

"Ha! Yes. There. You see? The old Sadyra. Already you make me wonder whether my offer is going to be another aggravation I don't need."

He shook his head and knelt before a two-drawered cabinet in the back corner behind the desk. Gathering up the discarded papers the cat had upset, he straightened them and methodically placed them into various slots within the bottom drawer.

Sadyra had to look away. The top of his breeks exposed more than she cared to look at. She muttered a term that described what the man needed to learn to wear, "Gitch."

The captain stiffened. He looked over his shoulder. "What did you call me?"

"Huh?"

"I heard you. You said my name. How do you know that?"

Sadyra spit out a laugh, but choked on it as the captain jumped to his feet and hovered over her; menace in his eyes.

"I fail to see the humour. You'd best be telling me where you heard my name, else Tural will be the least of your worries."

"Sorry. I had no idea. I was just…" She didn't know how to explain that she was making a rude statement about seeing his exposed backside.

The captain growled, one hand fingering the hilt of a plain handled dagger at his waist.

"I just thought that you should wear undergarments when you wear breeks like those." She shyly indicated his pants with her eyes and looked away.

"Undergarments?" He roared and pulled the dagger free—brandishing it in her face.

She leaned back against the wall but the dagger followed. "Yes, captain. Gitch."

He frowned and lowered the dagger. "Gitch? Is that what you said? I don't understand. What is, *gitch*?"

"Gitch is a slang term for undergarments. It's what me and my friends call them. I meant no harm."

The captain straightened and put his hands on his hips, looking out the window.

Sadyra could tell by the way his features twisted and scrunched that he was going over their conversation.

His eyebrows shot up. Turning to face her, his tanned cheeks reddened. "I see. I thought you called me by my real name."

He broke into a chuckle that quickly grew into a deep, belly laugh. Shoulders shaking and tears running down his cheeks, he had to hold onto the edge of the desk for support.

Sadyra was so tense, she couldn't help herself from laughing as well.

Together, they struggled to catch their breath.

"Oh...Sadyra..." The captain fought through his mirth. "You're gonna be...be the death of me!"

Scruff burst through the door, scimitar in hand. He mustn't have been far away. "Everything okay in here, Cap?"

The captain stopped laughing long enough to look at Scruff. He tried to say something but couldn't. Instead, he laughed louder than before; clutching Scruff's muscular shoulders and laying his bald head against the bewildered sailor's chest as he howled.

Scruff shouldered the office door aside, bearing three wooden plates piled with fish. He placed two on the desk amid three flagons of mead he'd fetched earlier.

The captain dismissed an old woman who had been tending to Sadyra's wound. The stoop-shouldered lady accepted a coin from the captain in her withered hand and squeezed her way out of the cramped office.

"Don't worry, I'll add it to your debt," the captain said to Sadyra before setting into his meal.

Sadyra rolled her eyes at the plate in front of her. "Great. Fish."

"Starve then," the captain said around a mouthful he had cut with his dagger.

She looked at Scruff standing in the corner, but he was too occupied with his meal. She estimated him to be six and a half feet tall—half a head taller than the captain. It was obvious he got his name from his unruly, black beard that stood out from his face as much as it hung down from his chin. It gave him the appearance of having an overly big head.

Succumbing to her hunger, she pulled her knife from its sheath and cut off a piece. It tasted better than it looked; practically melting on her tongue. "This is pretty good."

"Mm," the captain agreed, washing down a mouthful with a healthy swig. "Scruff here'll teach you the ropes."

Scruff stopped his knife loaded with fish from entering his mouth and gave the captain a hard look.

The captain raised his eyebrows. "You've something to say?"

Scruff growled, "Bad luck to have women onboard."

"Ha! Lack of women didn't help the *Catch*, did it?"

"That's different. The sea gods were angry."

"Angry with what?"

Scruff shrugged and bit the fish from the end of a rusty dagger. "The men ain't gonna like it."

"Tough. Tell them they'd better get used to it."

Scruff raised his eyebrows. It was obvious he wanted to protest some more, but kept quiet.

The animosity toward her inclusion in the captain's fishing gang wasn't lost on her.

Scruff wolfed down the last of his meal. "If ya ain't be needin' me, I'd like to join me mates at the *Cauldron*."

The captain speared the last of his meal and held his plate out to Scruff. "That's fine. Tell 'em they'd best keep a clear head come morning. We've got a busy day ahead."

"Aye, Cap." Scruff grabbed the captain's plate, took one look at Sadyra and grunted. "You gonna eat that?"

Sadyra forced herself to swallow the wad in her mouth. She nodded, afraid to speak to the intimidating sailor.

Scruff rolled his eyes, apparently waiting.

There was no way she could finish the plate in a hurry. Fearing to upset the man, she speared what remained with her knife and handed the plate to Scruff.

Scruff slipped from the office without another word. Pulling the door shut, he paused as the captain added, "I'll be along shortly."

"Aye, Cap." The door snicked shut behind him.

The captain must have noted how she looked at Scruff. "Don't worry about him. Oh, and by the way, don't fret over your father. I'll speak to him when he calms down. When he hears you're working for me, he'll back off. You'll see."

She mulled over his words as she set into another piece of fish. She didn't doubt the captain's intention, but she had trouble believing her father would listen to reason.

Trying to put her father out of her mind, she asked, "Is he always this pleasant?"

"Who? Scruff? Pretty much. But loyal to the bone. That man would stick a dagger in his eye before he allowed anything to happen to me."

"Fat lot of good he'd be to you then."

"Huh? Oh!" The captain laughed. "Aye. Just one of those speech figure things, or whatever you call them."

"So, when do I start?" She felt guilty sitting there, enjoying the captain's hospitality when she knew the danger her sisters were in. Hopefully the captain would keep his word.

"When? Why, you already have."

Sadyra hovered her fish laden knife over an upturned palm. "I haven't done anything yet."

"You've sat in my office for the better part of the evening."

Her eyebrows scrunched together.

"Anyone working for me gets paid for as long as they're within my building or manning my boats. Don't ever let me catch you saying Cap wasn't fair with you, you hear?"

"I haven't got that much seawater in my ears?"

"Huh?"

"Of course, I can hear you. I'm sitting right in front of you."

The captain held his breath, glaring at her with consternation. He exhaled and downed the rest of his mead.

"I think I'm regretting my decision already. Get outta here before I change my mind."

Sadyra gulped the remainder of her flagon, wiped her mouth on her shoulder, and unsteadily gained her feet. Her injured leg threatened to give out. She lifted and lowered it a couple of times, applying weight. It was painful, but she could walk.

She opened the door with her free hand and hobbled through.

"Sadyra."

She stopped and looked over her shoulder, wincing at the pain in her leg—her fish laden knife pointed at the captain.

"Be back by sunrise—no later."

Sadyra smirked. "Aye, Captain Gitch."

She managed to close the door fast enough to avoid being hit by a hastily flung flagon.

Sadyra

The Crew

Scruff was the first face Sadyra met the following morning, which wasn't surprising as she had learned that both he and the captain lived in the warehouse. She made sure she arrived at the fishery well before the sky lightened behind Peril's Peak. She jerked backward as the gruff man stepped from the shadows beside the door.

"Good morning." Sadyra tried to sound cheerier than she felt, but her greeting was lost on the sailor. In the faint light of the moon reflecting off the ocean, he ran his tongue inside his upper lip and looked away—settling his back against the wooden wall.

She made to go around him, but one look at his grizzled mien told her to wait. Swallowing her discomfort, she stepped back and forth, watching the lazy surf lap incessantly on the gravel shore while hugging her arms around her to ward off the morning chill.

The events of the previous night flitted through her mind. After leaving the fishery, she went straight to Bano's. To her relief, and surprise, her father hadn't gone there. Fearing it was only a matter of time before he showed up, she had remained awake well into the night, sitting on the floor with Bano beside her as her sisters slept in his cot.

Bano mentioned that his parents weren't keen on him harbouring Tural's children beneath their roof, but with Bano's persuasion, they had agreed.

She had woken with a start a short while ago, disturbed by a dream in which she ran forever but couldn't escape the demon chasing her. It wasn't the first time she'd dreamt this, but it *was* the first time the demon had gotten close enough to brush her skin with its claws. Her shivers increased at the thought.

She wasn't sure what bothered her more. The recurring dream, or the fact that she had awoken with her head resting against Bano's shoulder.

She sighed. Other than his penchant for ogling her, making her feel uncomfortable, and his annoying way of showing up unannounced to spend time with her when she'd prefer to be alone, Bano wasn't such a bad sort. It wasn't his fault her parents had betrothed him to her without her consent. She could almost justify the sense of possessiveness he held toward her since that announcement. They were to be wed on the spring equinox—the Mating Festival.

Her skin crawled. Not if she could help it.

"Ah, Sadyra!"

The captain's voice made her jump. Usually a very alert person, the man had snuck up behind her with a small torch in hand.

He strode past her and entered the fishery, smelling of acrid smoke and something that smelled even more repulsive but she couldn't put a name to.

He lit a sconce just inside the doorway and unlocked his office door with a large, rusted key. Sparking a flame to a candle on his desk, he handed the torch to Scruff who had followed on his heels.

Sadyra stood on the threshold of the building unsure what to do; the pungent smell of brine and dead fish turned up her nostrils. She wondered where the captain had been so early in the morning, but didn't think it was polite to ask.

Scruff walked deeper into the warehouse, igniting sconces as he went. The cluttered floor of baskets, stools, and benches came to life in the eerie glow of flickering light.

Sadyra

The captain beckoned to her from the doorway of his office. "Come, come. I won't bite. At least not until the sun comes up."

She swallowed and squeezed past him, assuming her spot on the stool beside the door.

"Have you eaten?"

She shook her head.

"Scruff! Bring an extra bowl." That said, he closed the door and lit several other candles. Sitting behind his desk, he smiled a crooked-tooth grin. "There. It'll warm up in here quick enough, you'll see."

She forced a smile for his benefit.

He folded his hands together on the desktop, his gaze taking in her lap. "So, how's the leg? You seem to be walking around a little better this morning."

"It was stiff when I woke, but it's not bad now. Still hurts."

"I bet it does. Looked like a nasty gash. I trust Henga was helpful."

Sadyra had been seen several times over the years by the Fishmonger Bay healer. "Yes, thank you."

"Great. I love that woman. Rumour has it she's older than the rest of the village put together." He leaned over his desk and whispered, "I have it on good authority that she's descended from elves."

Sadyra looked behind her at the closed door, wondering what prompted him to lower his voice. As far as she knew, the only one anywhere near the fishery was Scruff.

Playing along, she leaned in and whispered back, "I didn't think the elves had anything to do with Zephyr anymore."

The captain's face darkened for but a moment before the corner of his mouth turned up. He sat back and slapped the desk. "Ha! No wonder Tural wants to get his hands on you."

As soon as he said it, his face fell. "I'm sorry. That was harsh. I don't condone your father's actions, nor should I make light of them. Forgive me."

She held his gaze for a while to determine whether he was being genuine. "It's okay. I seem to have a way of irking people. I don't mean to. I just say what comes to mind."

"I told you we're alike. Perhaps in another life, we're related." His attention went to the door as it opened, admitting Scruff who balanced three steaming bowls.

Scruff deposited two on the desk, took a hard look at Sadyra, and exited the office.

"I don't think he likes me."

"Bah," the captain waved a hand at the closing door. "He's just upset you're sitting in his seat."

Sadyra jumped to her feet. "Oh. Sorry. He can have it."

She grabbed the door lever but the captain stayed her hand.

"No need. He'll get over it. Be good for him to eat with the crew for a change. Getting soft, that one."

"Soft?" Sadyra couldn't imagine Scruff being any harder than he appeared. "I'd hate to see him angry."

"Aye, lass. You're right there. Smash stone with his bare hands, that one. If you ask me, he's a giant runt, but he'll never admit it."

"A giant runt?"

The captain pulled a wooden spoon from the thick gruel and blew on it before putting it in his mouth and nodding his approval.

Sadyra fished her own spoon free and emulated the captain. Tasting the fare, her face scrunched up.

"Ya, it's not great, but I've had worse."

Sadyra stared at the contents on her spoon. "I haven't."

"Eat it or don't. No skin off my arse. Just know you won't be eating again for a while."

She put the spoon in her mouth and nibbled at the contents, unable to keep the revulsion from her face. It had the taste of dirt mixed with stale fish—tasting every bit like the warehouse smelled.

"Come on. Eat up. It'll put hair on your chest."

She gave him a disgusted look. “Ya, like that’s something I want.”

“It’d keep you warmer in the ocean breeze.”

“I’ll shiver, thanks.”

“Suit yourself. Anyway, getting back to Scruff. Long ago, in the age of dragons, humans weren’t the only ones inhabiting this forsaken region. Zephyr used to be part of a greater kingdom. Back then, it wasn’t uncommon to see an elf or dwarf, or even a giant. They weren’t from around Zephyr, but their kind did business with the old regime. As much as I believe Henga has elven roots, I also believe Scruff is descended from giants.”

“He’s big, but he’s not *that* big.”

The captain wrapped his lips around a spoonful. Pulling an empty spoon from his mouth, he pointed it at her. “Ah! That’s where you’re deceived. There are people taller than Scruff, that’s for sure, but I defy you to show me anyone half as strong. His strength isn’t natural.”

“Hmm,” Sadyra said trying to get a mouthful of gruel past her lips.

The outer door banged open and shut several times in quick succession.

“Anyway. Eat up. The crew’s arriving. As soon as we can see the reef, we’ll ship out.” He stood and used a thick finger to scoop at the residue on the side of his bowl. Sucking his finger, he smacked his lips in a mock gesture and went for the door.

Sadyra stood up, but he held out a staying hand.

“Please. Sit. Finish your breakfast. I’ll call for you when it’s time.” He didn’t wait for an answer.

She watched the door close and stretched her injured leg—wincing at the renewed stiffness that had taken hold of it. Wanting to keep it moving, she hobbled around the desk and peered through the filthy window, barely able to see the motley crew sitting around a couple of tables, shoveling slop into their mouths and laughing at something one of them had said. Their heads turned as one to regard the captain as he walked into their midst.

The largest man of the group, easily twice Scruff's weight, turned his red-bearded face toward the window and locked eyes with her. The way he stared didn't bode well for how she would be received by the crew.

Abashed, she turned away and wondered what she had gotten herself into.

The warehouse door banged many times. Sadyra approached the window. In the faint light streaming through the grimy windows spaced erratically along the walls, she observed Gitch's crew gather whatever implements they required from various places around the expansive room and file outside.

Her anxiety rose. It was time to mingle with a group of hardened sailors who openly detested the presence of a female when they took to the waves.

She took a deep breath. Perhaps Gitch's plan was to assign her a job in the warehouse. Cleaning fish, or packing them for villagers, and getting them ready for a southerly trip to Thunderhead and beyond.

The office door banged open. She jumped with a squeak.

Scruff poked his head in. "Ready, runt?"

She nodded, trying hard to hold his menacing gaze.

He stood with a muscular arm holding the door and motioned with his head. "Move. The boys ain't to be kept waiting."

Swallowing hard, she faked a smile and slipped through the door, painfully rubbing her body against the jamb to avoid touching the brute.

She scurried outside and stopped, not knowing what to do. Teams of three were loading shallow draft dories with fishing gear and pushing the craft down the gravel slope to the water's edge.

To a man, the sailors stopped what they were doing and glared at her. Time seemed to stand still until the red-headed man she had crossed stares with earlier, hocked and spat on the ground. He grumbled, saying something to the men around him. The men laughed, shook their heads, and went back to work.

The door opened behind her. Before she could convince her leaden legs to move, Scruff bumped her ahead as he exited the building, his arms full with netting and tack, and made his way toward the largest dory on the beach.

"Ah, there you are," the captain said as he rounded the corner of the warehouse. He motioned with an outstretched hand at the boat Scruff walked toward. "Time's a wasting."

"You gotta be kidding me," she said, her feet refusing to move.

"Bah. It'll be fine. I'll be with you. Come." He grabbed her behind the elbow and prodded her across the stony ground. "It's time you paid your debt."

She stopped well back of the dory and waited as Scruff mumbled to the captain; watching her out of the corner of his eye while stowing their gear.

"Well. Ya gonna push the boat out or are ya planning to become a figurehead?" Scruff snarled.

"Um, yes. Sure." She hurried to the boat, the bow facing inland, and placed her hands against its dark outwale. "Now?"

Scruff rolled his eyes. "No. Let's stand here for a while and enjoy the sunrise."

She ignored his sarcasm. Trying her best to forget about the pain in her leg, she pushed with everything she had.

The boat barely moved.

"Easy lass. You'll blow your back." The captain turned an exasperated look on Scruff, pointing to something on the ground she couldn't see. "Don't make this worse than it has to be. Stow the anchor."

Sadyra's eyes grew wide. She leaned around the end of the boat.

Scruff hoisted a rusted iron hook from where its considerable heft had settled in the loose gravel. The thick metal appeared to weigh nothing in his one-handed grip.

The boat rocked absorbing its weight.

"Now girl," the captain instructed.

Ignoring her slow building anger, Sadyra positioned her hands on each side of the pointed prow and put her back into it. The boat screeched forward a step but stopped. She drove her body into the boat, grunting and pushing, but it hardly moved.

Her breaths came in heaving spurts as she fell against the high bow. Peering around the curve of the outwale, she realized Scruff stood with his arms crossed, not bothering to help.

"Oh, I get it. Let's watch the stupid girl make a fool of herself." She leaned against the hull to catch her breath. "Well, you can damn well push it out yourself if you think you're so strong."

The boat lurched toward the shoreline—the sudden movement sent her tumbling to her side.

Laughter sounded all along the beach.

Biting back her mounting anger and disregarding her leg, she crawled back to her feet and tried to catch up to the fast-moving dory. She stumbled in her haste, not quite able to place her hands on the boat's hull until it splashed into the ocean and stopped. She jammed her cheek off the unforgiving prow.

Staggering backward with her hands on her face, she was aware of the crew enjoying her misfortune. Her face turned red. If she had a choice, she would have walked away and never come back. She sucked up her embarrassment. She had a debt to pay if she harboured any chance of keeping her sisters safe.

Sadyra

Scourge of the Catch

Pulling on the oars of Captain Gitch's over-sized dory was nothing short of back-breaking work. To make matters worse for Sadyra, the captain sat behind her in the bow, leaving her to face the brooding countenance of Scruff in the stern. She believed the obstinate man leered at her for no reason other than to let her know he wasn't the least bit amused that Gitch had not only allowed her to join their crew, but insisted she did so in their boat.

She did her best to ignore the furtive looks she received from the other boats within close proximity of their craft as they drifted on a northerly current. Her ears flamed hot every time she heard laughter, though she had no idea whether it was directed her way.

The morning had started out cool sitting in her wet clothing, but by the time she had rowed their dory beyond the reef and north along the shoreline, sweat beaded upon her brow. Anchored in the shadow of the massive overhang of the Summoning Stone, she stretched her cramping shoulder muscles.

Sadyra was no slouch when it came to rowing, but the family boat she was used to was much smaller. Scruff appeared to weigh more than her and her father combined. Nor did the captain's weight holding down the bow help matters.

"The storm's scattered the little buggers." The captain craned his neck one way and then the other, taking in the boats visible from where they bobbed on lazy swells. "The others don't seem to be faring much better."

Scruff's glare lingered on her. "Perhaps 'tis more'n the elements at play today."

If the captain heard, he made no indication. Staring at the ominous, projecting rock formation he said, "Weigh anchor and bring us into the shoals."

Sadyra's eyes widened. Scruff had cast the anchor into the ocean, but his lack of response told her it must be her job to bring it back in.

Grabbing the taut rope, she pulled and almost tipped over the inwale. She released the rope and caught herself on the boat's side, banging her knees on the ribbed strake.

"Easy lass or we'll be hauling you out of the sea." The captain's sudden movement to catch her by the elbow nearly upset the boat.

"Or not," Scruff mumbled, keeping his attention on the large net he pulled over the stern and piled at his feet.

A layer of water brought in with the net sloshed along the empty scuppers.

She cast Scruff a dark look, took hold of the rope, and inhaled deeply. Bracing her knees against the strake, she heaved and pulled the anchor to the surface—armlength by excruciating armlength, until its mass thumped on the hull.

Unsure she could lift it from the water and into the boat, she collected her reserves. Taking a deep breath, she regripped the rope at the water's surface and hauled the anchor into the boat, nearly dropping it on herself as she fell to her bottom with a splash.

A great roar escaped Scruff's bearded lips. He shook his head. "Good thing for you it didn't crack the hull."

She grabbed the rower's bench and pulled herself onto her seat. Cold water ran down her breeks and into her boots. Unable to keep her bitterness in check, she blurted, "Aye. Be a real shame to see you cast to the kraken."

Scruff stiffened.

"No harm done, lass. That old piece of anvil scrap is likely heavier than you. I'm amazed you lifted it." The captain settled into his seat. "Perhaps from now on, Scruff will handle it, hmmm?"

Sadyra swallowed; aware of the dirty scowl she received from the stern.

Sitting cross-legged, with her boots off, on a strip of sand immediately south of the Summoning Stone, Sadyra ate the meagre fare provided by one of the few boats that had managed to bring in a few fish. Soaked to the skin after jumping from the boat in the surf to help beach it, she shivered uncontrollably in front of a crackling fire of driftwood. Not daring to meet anyone's gaze, she kept her eyes on her boots lying between her and the flames.

Most of the men had stripped down to their breeks to allow the midday sun to warm their clammy skin. A couple of the more daring ones had taken off everything, caring little of her presence. For the most part, they spoke in groups; hushed words of the ill luck they had experienced this morning.

"Scruff," the captain's voice sounded somewhere behind her. "Walk with me."

Without looking up, she heard the swish of their damp leggings stride toward the base of the Summoning Stone.

At once, she sensed that the atmosphere around the fireside had changed. She kept her eyes down, but couldn't help overhear grumblings about her presence. She gritted her teeth. If she could find the strength to ignore them, she would be back on the water soon enough.

The brute with the red beard cleared his throat across the fire, hacking and spitting. A wad of spittle slapped the top of one of her sand-crusted boots. The thick mucus slid down the leather until it disappeared from sight.

His raised voice reached her across the fire. She feared to lift her gaze, dreading what she might see.

"Aye, wench. I'm talkin' to ye!"

Slowly raising her head, the red-bearded colossus glared at her; pointing a meaty finger her way.

"You tell 'er Slim."

Her eyes flicked to a clean-shaven, skinny man with slicked back, blonde hair. His nasally voice lisped through a partial set of yellowed teeth. She grimaced. He was one of the sailors strutting around naked.

Keeping her eyes averted as best she could, she studied the naked man's weathered face. It bespoke of a man much older than she had first pegged him for from afar while on the water.

Not intimidated by the older man, though his nakedness disgusted her, her anxiety made her blurt, "Why don't you tell me yourself, Slick?"

The men around the fire gaped and roared. A few repeated her nickname for their companion.

"Hah! Slick. That's a rich one."

"Ooh, a spirited one, eh…Slick!"

"Slick! That's what we'll call you from now on."

The smug grin slid from Slick's face. His eyes narrowed and his fists clenched. "Why you little tramp. I'll show you who's slick."

Sadyra scrambled to get up as he ran at her, scarcely able to stand before he wrapped wiry arms around her waist and drove her to the ground. She landed hard on her back, driving the wind from her lungs.

Howls of merriment sounded from all around.

"Get her Slick!"

"Tell the wench what she wants to hear!"

"Ye ha! Bust her one!"

Spittle flew from the corners of Slick's mouth as he straddled her waist and raised a fist high in the air.

Unable to catch her breath, she flinched, but the blow never landed.

Scruff slapped an iron-gripped hold on Slick's raised arm and lifted him flailing into the air. He dropped Slick to the side, and stepped back.

Slick stumbled and fell to his knees—baleful eyes finding Sadyra's but his attention was interrupted by the arrival of Gitch.

"That's enough! Who started this?" The captain hovered over Sadyra as she turned on her side and gasped painful, short intakes of breath. She couldn't speak.

Every sailor pointed at her.

The captain glared. "Is this true?"

She couldn't answer if she wanted to, but lying there, fighting to breathe, she decided it wouldn't do her any good if she disputed their claim. It was her word against theirs. She nodded.

"A fine way to ingratiate yourself into their company." He turned his attention on his men. "Prepare to cast off. We've got a lot of fishing to do to make up for this morning."

Shaking his head, he followed Scruff's broad back down the beach. His gaze lingered on Slick. "And for the serpent's sake, put your clothes on."

Sadyra sat up and watched everyone start for the boats. Many eyes lingered on her—none of them friendly. Exhaling a heavy sigh, she wiped her spit covered boot on a rock, banged the sand from them the best she could, and followed Scruff and the captain's footprints to where their dory lay partially beached.

The afternoon catch went little better than the morning. With the sun dropping to the steely horizon, Sadyra expertly guided the dory through the channel.

Sadyra

Her oar strokes slowed. She was in no hurry to get in.

Scruff growled, "You suddenly lose your strength? Get us in before the trolls."

She held his gaze but didn't respond. The phrase he used was a common way in Fishmonger Bay to say, 'before nightfall.'

"Take us to the pier," Gitch ordered, looking at the sky. "Looks like a calm night, so there's no need to beach."

Sadyra manoeuvred the over-sized dory behind another boat already tying off. The captain and Scruff threw ropes to men on the dock and exited the craft—not bothering to wait.

She remained in the boat and kept her head down to avoid the leers she felt from the departing sailors as they tromped by. More than once someone spat, but thankfully, they didn't hit her.

A voice she didn't recognize muttered as he trod past. "Scourge of the catch."

There was no mistaking who the words were aimed at.

Sadyra

Witch's Cauldron

The sun sank beneath the waves, taking the day's warmth with it. Soon the only sounds beside the incessant lapping of water breaking on the gravelly beach were the noise of Captain Gitch's boats pulling on their ropes, and the gentle swells slapping the pier stanchions in rhythmic cadence. The odd cry of a gull broke the still that had settled over the bay.

She studied a larger boat tethered to the far side of the pier. It wasn't from Fishmonger Bay. Whoever it belonged to, they didn't appear to have left someone behind to watch over it. But then again, this was Fishmonger Bay. The only real crime here occurred whenever a fight broke out—usually in the *Witch's Cauldron* after the fishermen had sated their need for mead.

Every now and then, the staccato of a door slamming in the village echoed off the towering cliff beyond the last row of buildings lining the commons. She cringed each time. The noise reminded her it was time to go home. Time to face her parents. No matter how she envisioned the meeting, no scenario ended well.

The far end of the jetty lit up as the door to the warehouse opened. She stared at whoever stood in the flickering light outlining the doorway, silently willing them to go away. It was hard to tell, but the person seemed to be looking her way. She bent low, so as not to be seen.

The door banged shut and for the briefest of moments she dared hope the person had gone back in, but the sound of gravel crunching underfoot, followed by footsteps clomping down the pier, told her otherwise. If it was Scruff, Slim or Slick, she was prepared to jump into the bay.

"Is that you, Sadyra?"

Relief washed over her. Captain Gitch was the least of her worries.

He stopped at the edge of the dock wearing a heavy sweater. "What're you still doing in the boat?"

She swallowed, not wishing to meet his gaze. Shivers of cold racked her body. "Freezing."

"I bet you are, you silly thing. Come on. Give me your hand and let's get you out of the cold."

Gitch held a hand down to her.

She ignored it at first, hoping he'd just go away, but when he didn't move, she sighed and allowed him to pull her from the dory.

The waves rolling against the jetty slapped and sprayed them as Gitch led her to shore. He stopped at the door to his warehouse and held it open. "Where are you going?"

His question slowed her steps. She stopped and looked back. "Home."

Gitch shook his head. "Nay. I can't let you leave before we get some food in ya."

She forced a smile. "I'm not hungry."

He raised his eyebrows, the warm glow from inside the building casting him in a serious light. "You work for me, remember? I'm telling you to get in here."

Sadyra looked away, trying to think of something to say to excuse herself. The last thing she wanted was to be around Gitch's crew. Given the alternative of facing her parents, perhaps it wasn't a bad idea. She dragged her feet across the gravel and entered the warehouse.

Gitch followed on her heels, closing the door behind them and motioning for her to enter the office. "Besides, what would your father say if he found out I let you starve?"

Sadyra was glad the captain couldn't see the shock on her face. "He'd likely pat you on the back and thank you."

If the captain heard her, he didn't let on. He hollered to someone in the warehouse, "Fetch us a bowl of slop," and squeezed by her to assume his place behind the cluttered desk.

She searched the ill-lit interior of the warehouse through the grimy office window—surprised not to see the crew sitting around the tables. The warehouse appeared empty.

The warmth of Gitch's office was a welcome relief to the bone-chilling temperature she had endured sitting in the boat. Wasting time here, however, only prolonged the inevitable. Truth be told, she'd rather get her confrontation over with. At this point, she didn't care how it turned out.

"So, how'd you like your first day?" Gitch folded his hands together on top of the papers on his desk.

She regarded him as if he had lost his mind. The day had begun with Scruff embarrassing her in front of the others. It had gotten worse when the naked man assaulted her. The afternoon had been insufferable when everyone realized that the catch wasn't getting better. From the reaction and mutterings of the crew, she knew they attributed their bad luck to her presence.

"It couldn't have been any better if someone had stuck a spear in my eye."

Captain Gitch nodded and smiled, but as her words sunk in, his face twisted into a puzzled expression.

"What? You honestly think that being mauled by a naked grandpa is something I enjoy?"

"No, but—"

"But what? You think I enjoy people whispering behind my back and spitting on me?"

Gitch's frown darkened. "Spit on you? Who did that?"

Sadyra held his stare; the smoldering anger in her eyes matching his, but she broke contact first. "It doesn't matter."

Gitch stood up and strode around his desk to lean over her. "Damn right it matters! No one treats my people that way. Tell me who did it and I'll run his arse outta town."

She came close to telling him who had spat on her boot while on the beach, but decided not to. Getting into a confrontation with Slim was the last thing she needed. She shook her head. "I'm not a rat."

Gitch stood over her, staring—his thick chest heaving.

The two of them jumped at the knock on the door.

The captain yanked the door open, poised to yell, but the sight of Scruff holding two bowls of steaming broth stopped him. He relieved Scruff of the bowls and the chunk of bread Scruff carried under his arm. "Go join the others. I'll be along shortly."

Scruff's intimidating gaze lingered on Sadyra. With a grunt, he turned and walked away. The exterior door banged shortly afterward.

Captain Gitch handed her a bowl and the bread, and placed the second bowl on the desk beside her. "They're both for you. Eat them up. You need to get meat on those bones."

He stepped through the doorway. "I'll be back. Don't leave until then. Understand?"

Sadyra stared at the bowl in her hands. For some reason, she felt like crying. She looked up and nodded at the man watching her with concern.

He appeared on the verge of saying something more, but simply nodded and left.

The exterior door banged and the warehouse fell deathly still. It was all she could do not to slip from the office and sneak into the night. The captain's generosity stopped her. Other than her sisters, she wasn't used to anyone caring for her. She sighed. There was also Bano, but she suspected an underlying motive behind his attention.

Left alone in the silent warehouse, unpleasant visions of her father and mother plagued her. She needed to get away from here. If not for the fear of her sister's safety, she would have left years ago.

The smell of the steaming broth pulled her out of her thoughts. It wasn't until she hesitantly tasted it that she realized how hungry she was. By the time the exterior door squealed open, she had devoured both bowls and soaked up the residue with the heel of bread.

"Ah. You're finished." Gitch smiled. "Good. I want you to join me at the *Cauldron*."

Alarm bells sounded in Sadyra's head. Fishmonger Bay only had one tavern and her father was a notorious patron. It would be bad enough facing him at home, but at least no one would see him hit her for wrecking the family boat. She'd be embarrassed if the villagers were to watch him beat her.

Gitch must have sensed her hesitancy. "What's the matter? You don't like ale?"

When she didn't respond fast enough, he said, "Ah, I see. It's my company, eh? Suit yourself. If you're worried I have ulterior motives concerning you, lassie, think again." He gestured to the darkened warehouse through the office window. "If that were on my mind, don't you think I would've already taken advantage of our situation?"

Shocked, Sadyra hung her head. The captain had been nothing but kind to her. "No, sir. It's not that, believe me. If it were, you'd be on the ground commiserating about the pain I inflicted on you."

Gitch considered her words. A wry smile crossed his face at the unspoken threat. "I don't doubt that. What is it then? The crew?"

Sadyra pursed her lips and tilted her head.

"Bah, you needn't fear them. They're just a bunch of fun-loving boys. They know where I stand when it comes to dissension amongst my people. If someone's bothering you, just say the word." He reached out and cupped her chin in his callused hand, lifting her gaze to his. "You hear me?"

She nodded in his hand, and pulled free of his hold. "It's not that. I need to confront my father."

She wanted to add that she feared for her sisters, but didn't want to bother the captain with her troubles. She stood. "I should go."

Gitch barred the doorway—not allowing her to exit. "I see. Well, if it makes you feel any better, I spoke to him last night. He was saddened that he killed you."

Sadyra gaped. She hadn't thought about what her father might have thought after she jumped into the ocean. She looked at the captain with wide eyes, a myriad of scenarios whirling around her head. If he thought she were dead…

"Don't get too excited. Once he got over the fact that you were alive, his mood started to drop again."

Sadyra felt the rising hope drain from her. "You told him I was alive?"

Gitch shrugged. "What else *could* I say? I couldn't very well allow the man to think he'd killed his child."

Sadyra sat down and muttered, "Dying would be the only thing I've ever done to make him happy."

Scratching his head, Gitch frowned. "Look. I know things between you and your pop ain't good."

She raised her eyebrows. "That's one way to put it."

"Ya. Well, whatever's happened between the two of ye, I'm thinking your meeting can wait. I just watched him stagger out of the *Cauldron* and head toward your cabin. If he makes it up the hill, I doubt he'll be in any shape to have meaningful words tonight."

Sadyra swallowed. The last place she wanted to be was facing her father's wrath when he was drunk. She had barely survived their last encounter.

She slapped her thighs and stood again. "It's okay, captain. I appreciate your efforts, but I'll never be one of the crew. I'm just working until I can earn enough money to buy my father another boat. Besides, I have no money for ale."

Gitch stared at her for a while. Finally, he nodded, a smile lighting up his face. "Don't cut yourself short. You're tougher than you give yourself credit. You're definitely a spirited lass—I'll give you that."

He leaned in to extinguish the sconce illuminating the office and gestured with an outstretched hand for her to precede him into the warehouse. “You just need to give the lads a chance. They’ll come around.”

He left her at the exterior door and went around snuffing out the last few sconces. Nodding for her to go outside, he closed the door behind them and put an arm around her shoulders, escorting her around the corner of the warehouse and steering her toward the *Witch’s Cauldron*. “As far as money goes, I’ll just add it to your tab.”

She stopped and stared.

Gitch laughed, impelling her across the commons. “I’m having sport with ya. Let me get the first round. After that…?” He shrugged.

She slowed their pace and looked him in the eye. She couldn’t detect anything untoward in his kind gaze.

“Come on, lassie.” His deep voice echoed of the cliff face in the deserted commons. “Time to ingratiate yourself with the crew.”

Being the only drinking hole north of Thunderhead, everyone from leagues around frequented the *Witch’s Cauldron* to unwind after a hard day’s work.

Sadyra had been in the one-roomed tavern several times, usually to fetch her father’s inebriated carcass on the request of one of the villagers before Tural got himself into more trouble.

Entering the *Cauldron,* escorted by Captain Gitch, raised more than a few eyebrows.

A surly bunch of sailors she didn’t recognize, crowded around a long bar lining one side of the large room, making a nuisance of themselves with the barmaids. Many of the young serving girls Sadyra had grown up with and hung around when she wasn’t required to work the family boat. Those days were infrequent over the last few years.

Used to such treatment, the barmaids forced themselves to laugh and fend off groping hands, going about their business as if everything was okay.

Sadyra glowered at the men watching her walk across the dirty, hardwood floor. A few winked. One blew a kiss.

Gitch snarled at the last man. Pulling on Sadyra's arm, he directed her to a group of tables in the back corner of the smoke-filled room.

The whole crew was there; each man regarding her with less than enthusiastic stares.

Slim nudged the older thin man with slicked-back blonde hair and weathered face, "Hey, *Slick*. Looks like your girlfriend has come for another romp."

Everyone roared and called out Sadyra's nickname for the man.

Slick's fists clenched and unclenched, a dour look on his face.

Gitch released her arm and pointed a finger in Slick's face. "Don't." He spun on Slim and raised his eyebrows. "And you…You should know better. Like it or not, Sadyra's a member of our crew." He glanced around to include everyone. "This goes for all of you. If I *ever* find out who spat on her, I'll run your sorry arse out of town. Is that understood?"

Grumbling and muttering met his admonishment, but no one said anything loud enough to be interpreted as a direct challenge.

"Do *not* take this warning lightly. As a crew, you're only as strong as your weakest link."

Everyone's eyes shot to Sadyra, but before anyone could say anything, Captain Gitch raised his voice. "And! I guarantee you sorry lot, that the weakest link ain't Sadyra."

Unhappy faces regarded their leader.

Slim grumbled, "But Cap, she's a woman."

Gitch's face turned purple. With great restraint, he kept his mouth closed. Nostrils flaring, he glared into Slim's green eyes, holding the tension for several breaths. When he spoke, it was through gritted teeth. “And you’re a man. What of it?”

Not deterred, Slim shrugged. “Just pointing out what they say about dames and boats, is all. Can’t blame the lads for that.”

“Silly superstition.” Gitch stepped away from the large man and motioned for his men to move over to clear a space for him to sit down. “And that’s the end of it.”

The captain whistled for a barmaid; circling his finger in the air to indicate a round for everyone. He patted the end of the bench for Sadyra.

An awkward silence fell over the crew. Two servant girls arrived bearing trays full of sloshing tankards. They seemed surprised to see Sadyra sitting with Gitch’s crew, but neither one said anything. They gave Sadyra a bashful smile and went about passing tankards all around.

“Put it on my tab, Frenza.” Gitch gave a crooked-tooth grin and winked at the blonde woman in a snug fitting, white tunic. Nodding at his crew, he said, “And let me know if any of these slugs give you trouble.”

Frenza gave him a slight curtsy. “Yes, Captain Opsigter. Your boys are never any trouble. I wish I could say the same for the crew out of Thunderhead.”

“Thunderhead, eh? That’s what I thought.”

“They got caught in the currents north of the Stone and couldn’t make it back before the trolls.”

Sadyra listened to her childhood friend. She hadn’t hung around with Frenza for years; only seeing her occasionally as they passed each other in town. She smiled at Frenza’s words. The ‘Stone’ meant the Summoning Stone, where they had put in at high noon.

How she missed her friends. If not for her father’s insistence that she take over the running of the family boat, she envisioned herself working at the *Cauldron* with her old mates. Her parents’ reliance on her to help with the family income—practically doing it herself in recent years—had her envying Frenza's simple lifestyle.

She watched her friend stroll across the tavern floor toward the far end of the bar, the woman's attire complimenting her shapely physique. As Frenza passed the group from Thunderhead, she squeaked and jumped sideways—cheeks red, as a large brute pinched her behind.

Sadyra stewed over her tankard, making note of the brown-bearded hulk and a few others who appeared to be the worst of the culprits. It gave her something to concentrate on while sitting with the crew. Other than the odd question or statement Gitch threw her way, nobody bothered including her in their conversation.

Downing her ale, she started to get up.

"Where're you going, lass?" Gitch put a rough hand on her forearm to keep her from walking away. "I've ordered you another."

"Oh no, captain. I can't let you buy me another one."

He raised his eyebrows, patting her hand. "Already done."

Sadyra sighed inwardly and sat back down.

Three tankards later, the ambience in the room started to swirl around her. Voracious voices filled the air, competing to be heard above the crowd that had crammed into the tavern—their words blurring into a dull roar. It was so loud, she could barely hear Gitch right beside her.

At one point, Scruff meandered over from the next table and motioned for the sailor sitting across from her to give up his seat. Scruff leaned in to talk to the captain about plans for the following day. The two men had to yell to be heard, but she could only make out snippets of their conversation.

Bored, she followed Frenza's movements around the room, admiring her old friend's patience when it came to dealing with the drunken patrons. Sadyra saw that Frenza was being tipped handsomely for her tableside manner, but she wondered at what cost.

Sadyra

Thinking about her earlier views of working as a barmaid, Sadyra came to the realization that perhaps being a barmaid wasn't the job for her. She didn't possess the patience to deal with the needy and rude customers demanding Frenza's attention.

The effects of the ale infused Sadyra with a warm glow. The tension she had experienced earlier at being thrust into hanging out in the *Cauldron* with a group of rough sailors who begrudged her inclusion in their tight-knit fraternity, eased from her mind. To hell with what they thought. She was in this for her, not them. If they didn't like it, too bad.

She smiled. She knew it was the alcohol talking but she didn't care. Ignoring the crew, her cheeks lifted in a great smile as she watched Frenza navigate the sea of people. How her friend did it without tiring, Sadyra had no idea.

Weariness set in. It had been a long day. Up before sunrise, and plying the oars beneath a hot sun all day, had sapped the energy from her. She crossed her arms on the table and laid her head down—letting the noise wash over her.

It was hard to keep her eyes from closing. It wouldn't do to pass out amongst a crowd of drunken sailors.

The sights and sounds in the *Cauldron* blurred together, hypnotizing her into a sense of comfortable numbness. As her eyelids drooped, threatening to take her to the fairies, she was vaguely aware of a white-bloused woman struggling to free herself from the attention of the brown-bearded hulk from Thunderhead.

As the relevance of who the woman was struck Sadyra, she lifted her head, fully alert.

Frenza was boxed in by three big men, allowing the brown bearded hulk a chance to reach his hands out and grasp her by the waist. Though his hands didn't seem to be doing anything more, the disgust on Frenza's face spoke plainly enough.

Sadyra

The floor skipped beneath Sadyra's feet as she stood and attempted to take a step toward the bar. She caught herself on the table; the effects of the alcohol hitting her hard.

Several of the crew laughed. She turned to see them watching her with interest, and smiled.

'Whoa, lassie. Where're you off to?" Captain Gitch grasped her arm to help steady her.

Sadyra's head lolled to the side. "Just…just over there." She pointed with the hand she had used to steady herself and fell back into the table—the impact sloshing ale from tankards.

"Hey!" a couple of men shouted, grabbing their drinks to prevent them from being spilled.

Sadyra grabbed onto the table again and raised her eyebrows. "Did the room just move?"

"Aye lass," Gitch laughed. "Darned near toppled our drinks." He patted the seat beside him. "Why don't you sit down again?"

"I got to—" A throaty belch escaped her lips. She faked an embarrassed smile and put her free hand to her lips. "I got to see my…" She staggered away from the table and burped again. "…my friend."

Gitch went to stand, but Scruff scoffed. "Let her go."

Sadyra took several uncertain steps forward, intermingled by the odd step sideways, and squeezed in between a Thunderhead sailor standing at the bar and the brown-bearded hulk who remained seated on a high barstool with his hands wrapped around Frenza's skinny waist.

The man she stepped in front of raised his eyebrows at her, about to say something, but a jab in the crotch from the end of Sadyra's knife cut his words short. She held a finger over her lips—raising her eyebrows and nodding toward the hulk.

She winked and withdrew the blade; whispering loud enough to be heard, "Watch this."

The man nodded and backed away, giving her room.

Sadyra

Frenza caught Sadyra looking over the brute's shoulder; fear clearly evident in the barmaid's round, blue eyes.

The brute had no idea Sadyra was behind him.

Ever so carefully, Sadyra lifted the back of his tunic and latched onto his old sword belt. With one hand holding the belt steady, she deftly applied her knife's razor-sharp edge. She had to be careful not the nick the pudgy rolls protruding over the belt, nor could she chance pulling too hard.

The priceless face on the man behind her made her snicker. Taking a deep breath, she paused until she stopped swaying, and resumed cutting the hulk's belt.

Frenza's startled gaze stared at Sadyra's head bobbing back and forth as she plied her knife.

The brute straightened his back and wriggled his shoulders. At one point he grabbed onto his sword belt and adjusted it, but his attention was focused on Frenza.

The knife jumped as it cut through the last bit of leather and Sadyra fell shoulder first against his back.

"Hey!" He released Frenza who took the opportunity to duck between the men hemming her in. He grabbed at his belt, the look on his face puzzled but seeing Sadyra's smiling face redirected his attention. "What the…Oh. Hey there. I haven't seen you before."

Sadyra latched onto his corded forearm to pull herself upright. She answered him with a wide, closed-mouth grin.

A great smile parted his thick, hairy lips. "And what do they call you, sweet girl?"

Sadyra swayed, but she held his bloodshot gaze. "Depends on how well they know me."

A sly grin and mischievous twinkle in his eyes, he said, "I be liking the sound of that, hey boys?"

He grabbed his tankard from the bar and clashed it against several others.

Sadyra held her hand out as he chugged his ale.

Sadyra

"I love this dame!" The man proclaimed for the whole bar to hear. He handed her his metal stein and opened his eyes wide in anticipation of Sadyra quaffing his ale.

The noise in the bar dropped off. Most of the patrons who weren't passed out or otherwise engaged in their own endeavours, stopped what they were doing to observe the spectacle.

Gitch had gotten up from the table and stood halfway across the room, concern on his face.

Sadyra brought the tankard to her lips, raising her eyebrows twice in quick succession.

The brute leaned toward her, urging her to drink, but his expression fell from his face as Sadyra swung the tankard out wide and smacked him in the temple so hard that the brim dented; cutting his brow and dousing him with a face full of ale.

The men from Thunderhead let out a collective gasp.

Sadyra tossed the tankard to the ground and staggered toward Gitch.

The brute held a massive hand to his face; pulling it away covered in blood. His evil scowl honed in on Sadyra. "Why you little tramp!" He stood; drawing his sword and stepping forward. As his sword cleared its sheath, confusion twisted his enraged features. The severed sword belt, attached to his breeks, dropped around his ankles and tripped him. His sword flew from his hand and slid across the floor as he tried to break his fall. His knees hit the floor hard—his bare backside exposed for all to see.

Laughter thundered throughout the tavern.

The man's guttural scream pierced the din. Rising to his feet, uncaring that his breeks were around his ankles, he struggled to extract his feet from their confines. His boots caught up in material, causing him to stumble.

He hung onto the arm of one of his crew and pointed; spit flying from his lips. "Get her!"

Gitch grabbed Sadyra and pulled her back to where his own crew were rising to their feet.

"No! Stop! No fighting!" A skinny man in an apron ran out from behind the bar but nobody paid attention to him.

The *Witch's Cauldron* erupted. Fists flew and bodies were tossed. Tables were overturned and stools were smashed across backs.

A tankard clanged off the wall beside Sadyra's head, spraying her and Gitch with warm ale.

Gitch glared. "Look what you've done."

Sadyra gave him a contented grin, her upper body swaying back and forth. "He had it coming."

"*He* had it coming? The whole place has gone crazy." Gitch shook his head. "You get this from your father."

The colour drained from Sadyra's face. She put her forehead against the captain's. "You take that b…b…" she belched the rest of the word, "…aaaaack."

Gitch sighed, clearly not happy. He pulled Sadyra out of harm's way as an errant chair shattered on the wall where she had just stood.

One of the Thunderhead sailors approached with a table leg in hand.

Gitch moved to intercept him—ducking the man's swing at his head, and driving his shoulder into him. They fell away and were swallowed by the chaos.

Sadyra's head felt thick with wool. In the ensuing bedlam it was difficult to concentrate on any one person as the fisticuffs evolved into an all-out brawl.

She caught sight of Slick squaring off with someone who appeared to be out of his league. She looked forward to seeing him eat a fist but movement behind the older sailor drew her attention.

Another man from the Thunderhead contingent walked up behind Slick with a broken stool in hand. The man nodded at the bigger fellow confronting Slick and hoisted the stool over his head.

Sadyra

The people around Sadyra flew by in a blur as she sprinted across the space separating her from Slick. She left her feet; diving at the man hoisting the stool. She crashed into one of his upraised arms, her momentum driving the two of them over a table littered with flagons and wooden plates. The chair smashed harmlessly to the hardwood floor.

Sadyra slid across the table on top of the man until their weight overbalanced its far end and they tumbled to the ground beneath a shower of uneaten food and drink.

The addled sailor shook his head, surprise on his face as he looked into the freckled visage of Sadyra smiling down at him. Sadyra punched him in the side of the face so hard that his tense body went slack beneath her. She had knocked him out.

She cupped her hand, conscious of the blood seeping from her knuckles. The man's face had cut her fingers. She poised herself to hit him again to vent her frustration of injuring her fist, but a pair of hands grabbed onto the back of her tunic and hoisted her into the air; throwing her against the wall beyond the man she had taken down.

Her breath left her as she impacted the unforgiving wood and slid down its rough surface into a crumpled heap on the floor; barely conscious. Dazed, she saw that it was the brown-bearded brute who stood over her—his sword belt missing and his breeks pulled up around his waist. He growled and bent forward.

His hands never reached her. An impatient anger twisted his features as he spun to stare into Scruff's unruly, black-bearded face. He raised a fist and threw it. "This don't concern you!"

Surprise replaced the hulk's anger. Scruff avoided the punch and latched onto his upper arms; lifting the man off the floor.

Sadyra tried to concentrate. The hulk must have weighed three times her weight, but the way Scruff spun and pitched the man across the room into a group of sailors facing off with Gitch's crew made it seem like the brute weighed no more than a small dog.

Scruff, Slim, Gitch and several others Sadyra knew only by looks, corralled the last of the Thunderhead crew and escorted them from the tavern.

Sadyra wasn't sure how long she sat slumped against the wall but as her senses came back to her in a moment of lucidity, she realized that the sailor she had taken down no longer lay by her feet. Looking around, most of the people were gone and the noise in the great room had diminished to casual conversation.

Wood scraped across the floor near the bar. The skinny man with the apron righted an upturned stool and examined it. Shaking his head, he tossed it into a growing pile of broken furniture in the middle of the floor.

The enormity of what had transpired weighed on her. Because of her actions, the interior of the *Witch's Cauldron* had been sacked. Several people sat on benches nursing bruises and cuts. Frenza and her workmates were busy picking up discarded cutlery and earthenware; sweeping shattered debris and righting tables.

Sadyra struggled to hold onto consciousness. The scene unfolding in the room spun in lazy circles before her eyes. The more she watched, the more she felt like throwing up. As her eyes closed, she thought she saw one of the barmaids watching her. Frenza put aside her broom and came her way.

The next thing Sadyra remembered was a soft voice calling her name—cold fingers holding her face.

"She'll be alright. Let her sleep it off," a male's deep voice sounded from somewhere nearby. "I'll take her from here."

A thick arm slid behind her neck and another collected her legs together. She had the sensation of being lifted. Her head lolled to one side and a heavy musk scent filled her nostrils, but she didn't have the wherewithal to open her eyes and see who had her in his arms.

Heavy boots trod across hardwood flooring. Hinges squealed and a blast of cold air hit her—a welcome relief to the heat of the bar.

Sadyra

Seaside Antics

How Sadyra got from the *Witch's Cauldron* to Captain Gitch's office, she had no idea. The last thing she remembered was sitting in the *Witch's Cauldron* with the crew, watching Frenza scurry about the bar.

Squinting in the flickering glow of the sconce burning on the wall, she lifted her head and winced. It felt as if someone had stuck a dagger in her temple and twisted it.

"Ah. If it ain't the *Cauldron* brawler herself."

Sadyra blinked several times, trying to clear the cobwebs from her brain. She pushed herself into a sitting position; leaning her head against the wall between the seat she usually occupied and Captain Gitch's desk. She opened her eyes wider, attempting to clear her fuzzy vision.

Gitch leaned his balding head across his desk and smiled. "That was quite a night."

Sadyra tried to swallow but her mouth was too dry. She clenched her left fist; grimacing at the pain. Inspecting her damaged hand, she groaned, "What time is it?"

"High time we get some gruel into us and prepare the boats. The rooster's a-crowing."

The warehouse lay in darkness beyond the office window. She closed her eyes; afraid she might throw up if she moved.

Gitch walked around the desk and opened the office door. Cold wafted across the floor, raising goosebumps all over her body.

"Hey!"

The captain's loud voice grated in her skull.

"A round of slop!" He closed the door and looked down at her. "That was some performance last night."

Her head rolled to the side, gazing up at the man through one, partially opened eye. "What happened?"

"Hah!" Gitch clapped his hands together, the sudden noise making her cringe. "Other than starting a war with a rival crew and tearing down the *Cauldron*, not much."

The events seeped into the forefront of her thoughts. An image of the brown-bearded brute gaping at her with his breeks around his ankles made her chuckle momentarily, but the action caused her head further agony.

Gitch sat behind his desk and sighed. "Looks like you'll be working for me a good while longer."

She frowned and rolled her head to look at him through bleary eyes.

"Gonna take a fair bit of coin to repair the damage you caused."

"Me?"

"Aye. According to witnesses, you were the instigator."

She forced herself to swallow the little saliva she could muster. "I was helping Frenza escape the clutches of that Thunderhead troll."

Gitch shrugged. "Whatever. Doesn't change the fact that you're on the hook for the damages."

"Why me? I didn't break anything."

"That's the way it works. You start the riot. You pay for the outcome."

Sadyra rolled her eyes and closed them to fend off the light. She mumbled, "What's it going to set me back?"

Gitch whistled. "Don't know, yet. A far cry more than you owe me, I can assure you that."

She sighed, trying to find a way to position her head in such a way to reduce the ache, but nothing helped.

A rap on the door startled her.

Careful not to step on her legs, Gitch opened it, admitting Scruff.

Scruff stepped over her and put two of the three bowls of steaming gruel he carried on the desk. Keeping one for himself, he pulled the door closed and assumed the chair Sadyra usually sat in. “I see the runt’s alive.”

Gitch retook his seat and dug into his breakfast, speaking around a mouthful. “Aye. Feeling worse for wear but she’ll live.”

Scruff grunted.

The sound of the exterior warehouse door opening and closing with a bang over the next little while made Sadyra jump each time someone entered the building.

Scruff wiped the remnants of his breakfast from his bearded lips and nodded at Sadyra. “Looks like we’ll be needing a third this morning.”

“Bah!” Gitch banged his bowl on the desktop. “She’ll be fine, won’t you Sadyra?”

Sadyra lolled her head along the wall to stare at the captain’s wide grin. She didn’t dignify him with an answer.

“Seems like it,” Scruff muttered getting to his feet. “I’ll get the boat ready.”

“Watch the Thunderhead crew don’t give you any trouble.”

Scruff stopped on the threshold and grunted. “Already spoke to their captain. Said they were shoving off before sun up. He wanted to have words with the runt, but I told him that wasn’t happening.”

“Surf’s calm, I take it?”

“Aye, they’ll have no trouble sailing through the gap.”

“Good enough. Let me know when the lads are ready. I’ll see to little Miss brawler.”

Scruff lingered on the threshold, staring at Sadyra.

She opened one eye and looked back.

He grunted and left the office.

The door slammed in his wake. She cringed; sure he had done it on purpose.

Sadyra

Pulling on the oars tested Sadyra in many ways she wasn't accustomed to, but after the initial, agonizing first part of the morning, her hurts and aches subsided to tolerable levels. The pain of salt spray on her raw knuckles helped her forget her splitting headache.

She had originally feared that the large boat out of Thunderhead would catch their fleet on the open water. That's all she needed was to have Gitch's crew blame her if things turned sour on the ocean swells, but by the time they rowed beyond the gap in the reef and had a clear view of the coast, the boat was nowhere in sight.

Her shoulder muscles ached from yesterday's fishing excursion and Scruff made no bones about complaining about their progress.

"If you pull any slower, the tide will take us to the drop-off."

She cast him an exasperated glare, but was too exhausted to rise to the bait. The fabled drop-off meant the edge of the world. There was no way she was going to allow that to happen. The boat was moving—perhaps not keeping up with the rest but who was to say the waters they languished in contained less fish?

With sun beaming straight down, they dropped anchor and bobbed on the ocean about a league north of the Summoning Stone. The crag infested waters along the shoreline made beaching impossible so they stopped upon the waves for their midday meal. The morning had proven better than yesterday and several buckets were full of fish.

Even at that distance, the ominous black rock ledge dominated the shoreline. Just the sight of it made Sadyra shiver. The Summoning Stone signified the upcoming celebration. One that she dearly wished she wouldn't have to partake in. Her parents had proclaimed that she and Bano were to wed at the Mating Festival—thus bonding her to him.

She gritted her teeth and stared at the water sloshing about the scuppers, fighting back tears. In the grand scheme of things, perhaps becoming Bano's mate would prove a godsend. It would free her of her family's obligation and get her out from underneath her parents brooding shadow.

She sighed. They would turn their drunken ire on Sleena and Sable.

Scruff grunted from the stern. He held out two large pieces of raw fish.

She frowned.

"Are you gonna take it or not?"

She accepted the fish and forced a smile. "Thanks."

Tentatively tasting one, she nodded. Scruff had sprinkled some kind of seasoning on them.

"Give one to Cap, you stupid runt."

Any thoughts of having made inroads with the crew evaporated in the time it took Scruff to berate her.

The afternoon went much like the morning. Sadyra's headache was replaced by blistered palms that broke open. Gritty seawater stung the raw flesh, but she refused to complain. It wouldn't do her any good.

As the sun dropped low in the western sky, the incoming tide pounded the base of the Summoning Stone as they made their way south toward Fishmonger Bay.

The captain followed her gaze up to its dizzying height. "Ah. The old mating rock. Many a fine maiden has lost her virtue up their…oh."

Gitch's cheeks reddened. "I beg your pardon. I forget myself."

"Pfft. Please." Scruff hocked and spat—the wad arching high and far over the water. "If the runt wants to be a member of the crew, it's time we started treating her like one."

Without warning, he stood up and relieved himself off the back of the boat.

Good-natured jibing sounded over the waves from the men floating nearby.

Sadyra looked away, her cheeks turning colour.

A sudden urge took hold of her. If she had taken the time to think about it, she would never have followed through.

Scruff stood on a thin bench in the stern, his back to her; knees bent to absorb the roll of the ocean.

Sadyra could see the stream between the gap in his legs. A mischievous grin lifted her cheeks. She dipped the oars into the water and pushed on the handles enough to stutter the boat's forward momentum and then pulled for all she was worth.

The dory lurched forward.

"Heeeey!" Scruff cried out and pitched over the back of the boat with a large splash.

"What the…" Gitch leaned on Sadyra's shoulders trying to locate Scruff in the water.

Laughter echoed off the Summoning Stone as the occupants of every boat within hailing distance pointed and held their stomachs in various states of hysterical laughter.

Sadyra returned the captain's inquisitive stare with a sly smile.

Gitch's eyes widened, his clean-shaven face full of wonder. "You didn't?"

Her demure grin was answer enough.

He looked to where Scruff struggled to hang onto to his breeks while keeping his head above the waves, and then looked back at her.

Sadyra had to release an oar and lean to the side to avoid the captain as he fell into the water-logged scuppers, howling uncontrollably.

Sadyra

The tension of the last few days eased from Sadyra's troubled mind. She released the other oar and fell onto her back beside the captain, laughing hard.

"He's...he's...he's gonna..." Trying to speak through his laughter, Gitch spit out, "Kill you!"

The gravity of what she had done slapped her in the face. She sat up and stared at Gitch, her face full of fear. Swallowing her dread, she watched as Scruff swam for all he was worth. Unable to control herself, she said quickly, "He's got to catch us first!" And dropped to her back, howling, despite the trouble she was in.

Gitch sat up and held her stare long enough to listen, before his laughter echoed off the cliffs as he joined her in the bottom of the boat.

Sadyra

Learning the Ropes

Sadyra's fingers bled. If she had to mend one more net, she thought she might scream. Hazarding a glance at the dark scowl twisting Scruff's features, she was thankful that it hadn't gone any worse than it had. Another boat had plucked the surly sailor from the waves. If not for Captain Gitch's intervention, Sadyra was certain Scruff would have flayed her alive when they met again.

To help mollify the irate Scruff, Gitch had ordered Sadyra to clean and repair all of the crew's gear while they were excused to go home for the day.

Scruff demanded permission to watch over her to ensure she didn't shirk her punishment. Gitch had reluctantly agreed after making Scruff promise not to lay a hand on her.

"Gonna be here all night at this rate," Scruff growled at one point; his bulk looking uncomfortable on the low tree stump he sat on.

Sadyra bit back a smart reply that begged to escape her lips. Even though he had assured the captain that he wouldn't touch her, she doubted it wouldn't take much to push the sodden sailor over the edge.

Darkness settled over Fishmonger Bay—the evening hours stretching into night.

Scruff planted two torches in the gravel to give Sadyra enough light to see.

Her stomach pained her something fierce. Seated cross-legged on a small boulder, she wondered how the large man could sit there all night and not eat. Surely, he was hungry.

As the night wore on, members of the crew crunched across the gravel commons to see how they were making out. A few ales to the wind, the braver men like Slim, slapped Scruff on the back, enjoying themselves as they regaled in the story of his inglorious dive into the ocean while in the midst of relieving himself.

No one paid attention to Sadyra other than to glare and shake their heads.

The moon shone high overhead as Sadyra grabbed the last of the heavy nets and started pulling seaweed from its loops. Searching for holes, her stomach twisted painfully. She studied Scruff's hairy profile in the flickering torchlight. "Aren't you hungry?"

If he heard her, he made no sign.

She lowered the net to her lap and sighed. "Why do you hate me?"

Scruff seemed to breathe a little heavier. He licked his lips and turned a dark look her way, but didn't say anything.

"I haven't done anything to…" She raised her eyebrows and emitted a nervous chuckle. "Well, other than…you know."

She swallowed. This wasn't going well. She could tell he struggled to restrain himself from saying or doing what was on his mind. And yet, she persisted. "I don't understand what sailors have against women on boats."

"It's bad luck." The fact that he responded at all, shocked her.

"But why?"

He shrugged. "Just is."

"That makes no sense. There has to be a reason."

His stone-faced glare made her shiver. She was sure he was done talking when he turned to look out at the dark purple-hued waves lapping the shoreline—each wave receding a little more with the lowering tide. "Don't rightly know. It's what I've been taught, so that's the way it is."

Sadyra mulled over his answer. “Just because someone says something, doesn’t make it true.”

Scruff chewed on his lower lip but said nothing.

“It’s a silly superstition, if you ask me.”

Scruff grunted. “Ain’t no one asking.”

Sadyra felt her temper surfacing. She took a deep breath and turned her attention on the net—moving it around with sudden jerks. The sooner she got it done, the sooner she’d be able to…

Her shoulders slumped. Returning home, especially this late at night, didn’t fill her with much hope that her night would get any easier.

“The boys aren’t happy, but they’re moving,” Scruff said to the wind.

Stewing over the unfairness of it all, Scruff’s words startled her. Did the crew actually despise her that much? Trying to make sense of what he said, she asked, “Moving? Where are they going?”

His heavy brow came together. “What are you talking about?”

She hesitated, almost afraid to continue. “You said the boys were moving.”

He shook his head. “You really *are* something. I meant their feelings about your place in the crew is changing.”

Sadyra’s eyes widened, daring to hope.

“Slowly, mind. I don’t think they’ll ever get used to a dame on the waves, but your actions last night opened a few eyes.”

She swallowed. From what she remembered, her drunken actions were far from a glowing testimony as to how she had handled herself. Staring into Scruff’s large, brown eyes she dreaded what she had done once the fight was over as she still had no recollection of anything afterward. One moment she was flying through the air at the man hoisting the barstool and the next she had found herself sprawled on the floor in Captain Gitch’s office.

Scruff hocked and spat toward the shoreline. "Putting yourself on the line to save *Slick*." He smiled as he used her nickname for the old sailor. "Especially after he attacked you on the beach. If I'm not mistaken, you've elevated a few of the lads' opinion of you."

She nodded, goosebumps running up her neck.

"You also stood up to one of the toughest men in the bar. That shows you got spunk, and that will go a long way with the crew." He raised his eyebrows and looked her in the eye. "Either that or you're stupider than I've given you credit for."

The growing warmth inside her was curtailed by his last statement.

Gravel crunched from the direction of the warehouse. Captain Gitch strolled toward them with a handheld sconce.

Scruff stood to greet the captain, but his muttered words were meant for her, "Watch your step, runt. Don't push it. There's hope for you, but…" He turned a dark gaze on her. "Try something like what you did to me again, and I'll see that you never take another step."

"Ah, it's nice to see you two are getting along," Gitch said as he stopped before Scruff.

Scruff grunted.

"How's she doing?"

"Making a career of it."

"Ah, well, why don't you make your way to the *Cauldron*? I'll stay with her."

"It's open?"

"Aye. For the crew it is. You might have to stand though." Gitch chuckled and motioned with his head toward the commons. "Go."

Scruff grunted and tromped into the night.

The captain sat on the vacated tree stump and examined the piles of netting. "Almost done?"

She forced a smile and lifted the edge of the heavy net on her lap. "Last one."

"Good. Good." He craned his neck to watch Scruff's progress until the man disappeared into the *Witch's Cauldron*. He turned back to her. "No trouble?"

"With Scruff? No."

"Good. Good. He's a good man, that one. A little rough around the edges but his head's on straight."

Sadyra raised her eyebrows. "A *little* rough?"

Gitch smiled. "Okay. A lot, but there ain't a better man to watch over the business. That's why I employ him. Not as a fisherman, though he's learned to become one. I found him years ago, way down in Ember Breath of all places."

"He's from there?"

"Don't know. When I found him, he was on the run from someone. Someone important, if I have the right of it. He never speaks of his past and I never inquire. He does his job watching over me and my business and that's all I ask."

Sadyra nodded.

Gitch's smile left his face. He stared out over the dark water. "Gonna hate to lose him."

"Where's he going?"

"Not sure. Every now and then he tells me that he needs to make amends." Gitch shrugged. "Whatever that means. I could be wrong…Hope I am, actually, but I fear one of these days he's gonna follow through with it."

Sadyra didn't know what to say. She put her mind to finish clearing the last net of debris, hoping she wouldn't come across a tear in the coarse weave.

"He doesn't like me very much," she mumbled, more to herself.

Gitch leaned toward her. "What's that?"

"Nothing."

"You don't think who likes you? Scruff?"

Sadyra set the net in her lap and sighed. "Ya. Well none of them, really, but especially Scruff."

"Pitching him to the krakens probably wasn't a great idea."

She hung her head, but looked sideways to see a genuine grin on the captain's face.

"I have to admit, it *was* funny," Gitch chuckled. "But don't tell Scruff that."

"I won't."

"With regard to him not liking you, I wouldn't worry too much about it. He doesn't like many people. I doubt he likes himself. But," he held up a finger. "I think you're wrong about how he feels about you."

She frowned.

Gitch nodded. "Aye. If anyone else had done what you did to him, I doubt even I could have prevented him from shanking them."

"Probably because I'm a girl," Sadyra turned her attention back to the net, though she was in no hurry to finish the job.

The captain raised his eyebrows. "No. That's not it. Scruff couldn't care less about your sex, trust me. In case you haven't noticed, he's made no bones about your presence in the crew."

"Ya, him and everyone else."

"That being said, from what I've seen, especially after last night, he's fonder of you than you think."

Sadyra frowned at the unspoken implication.

"If nothing else, I think he has begrudgingly gained a new respect for you."

"Got a strange way of showing it."

"If you're expecting gushing praise and warmth from that one, good luck. He's as cold as the Summoning Stone."

Sadyra flinched at the mention of the detested jut of rock.

"In all the years I've known Scruff, I've never once known him to share his meal with anyone. Well, except me, of course."

Sadyra frowned deeper.

"The fish he offered you in the boat. I've never seen him do that."

"Big deal. He yelled at me as soon as he handed it to me. Probably mad at himself for slipping up."

"Perhaps." The captain shrugged. "That still doesn't account for what he did after the bar fight."

Sadyra shuddered. She felt she might be better off not knowing, but she couldn't help herself. "And what's that?"

She could tell by how he stared at her that the captain debated whether he should tell her or not. She leaned forward. "Well?"

"He carried you from the *Cauldron* and insisted that I show him where you live. I didn't think you'd want to be taken home, so I opened my office and he put you in there."

Sadyra thought about it. He probably wanted to get her out of the way.

"I guess you could say, in a roundabout way, your antics at the tavern were a positive step toward learning the ropes of being part of the crew. You initiated the brawl, but you didn't back away when things turned bad." He nodded to her. "And that, Sadyra Ors, will go a long way to helping the boys accept you into their fold."

She contemplated his explanation. Being part of the crew was apparently more complicated than just fishing. She sighed. It made no sense that in order to be accepted, one had to get their head kicked in. She never understood the ways of men.

"Anyway, don't think they'll treat you any differently than before." The captain stood and collected the first of the many nets. Holding it in his arms he nodded to the warehouse. "Leave that one. I'm sure it's fine. I'll help you lug them in."

Sadyra allowed herself a faint smile. "I'd appreciate that."

Folding the heavy net the way she had seen the crew do it, she struggled to carry the bulky weight in the captain's footsteps.

Gitch didn't appear to have any trouble at all. He slowed to allow her to keep pace. "You know what else Scruff did?"

"Do I want to know?"

"He offered…No. He *demanded* to remain with you all night to ensure that no one…um…you know? Tried to take advantage of your condition."

She stopped and gaped.

Gitch kept walking. "Aye. He even fetched you a blanket from his bunk in the warehouse."

She scrambled after him; constantly readjusting her grip as the net tried to slip out of her arms. "You're kidding, right?"

"Not at all. He was adamant. If I wasn't so drunk, I would've thought I had even seen compassion in his eyes." He raised his eyebrows, giving her an intense look. "Do *not* tell him I said that."

"I don't recall having a blanket."

"That's because he took it from you when he determined it was time you faced the day."

Stunned, Sadyra didn't say anything else while they put the nets away. By the time they were finished, she didn't think she could take another step. Gitch had found them half a loaf of stale bread and some cheese. They ate in relative silence.

Wolfing it down and chasing it with foul-tasting wine Gitch had boasted about making himself, Sadyra brushed the crumbs from her lap and walked out of the office.

"Where to now?" Gitch asked as he pulled the warehouse door closed and stepped into the moonlight.

"Home. I guess," Sadyra said with a sad voice.

Gitch placed an arm around her shoulders and gave her a reassuring smile. "Come. I'll go with you. It'll be okay. You'll see."

Sadyra

Going Home

Going home didn't seem nearly as bad with Gitch by her side. Though, tired as she was, the steep climb tested her endurance. She stopped three times to rest—partly due to fatigue and partly out of fear of what was to come. She hadn't seen her family for a few days—ever since her father had chased her into the ocean.

They turned up the small path leading to the cabin. Gitch strode behind her. "Do you think they'll be awake?"

Depends how much booze they've drank, she thought, but kept it to herself. "Probably."

"Now remember. I had a heart-to-heart with him the other night. If he doesn't bring it up, I wouldn't either."

Sadyra took in Gitch's words but didn't respond—her mind too preoccupied with the whirling emotions that confronting her parents brought out in her. With her parents—Tural in particular—she never knew where she stood. Nor could she forget that the last words she had with her mother had been at knifepoint.

Stopping before the thin porch that had needed replacing for as long as she could remember, Sadyra raised her eyebrows at Gitch. Swallowing her discomfort, she let out a long breath and pulled the cabin's only door open—the squeal of neglected hinges piercing the night.

A single candle flickered on the right side of the one-roomed hut; shedding poor light on the pallet against the wall.

"Who's there?" Tural's deep voice grated.

"It's just me, Father."

"Sadie?" Her mother's voice chimed in. "Thank the gods, you're home."

Sadyra rolled her eyes for Gitch's benefit. Her mother always acted this way after they had a fall-out—begging for forgiveness and often breaking into tears of false remorse.

A large shadow rose from where the pallet lay in shadow. "Who's that with you?"

"Captain Gi—" Sadyra caught herself. "The captain wanted to see me home. You know? Trolls and all."

Tural emerged into the candlelight wearing nothing but a bedsheet. He nodded. "Much obliged, captain. I'm sorry she's a bother." He lit another candle and placed it on the table, calling over his shoulder as he did so. "Areeza. Fetch the good captain something to drink."

Areeza's naked silhouette scrambled to pull a smock over her head. She walked into the candlelight looking like death warmed over, reeking of wine; her squinting eyes bloodshot.

"Have a seat." Tural pulled out a rickety chair for the captain and one for himself.

"Sadie?" a small voice inquired from the far side of the cabin where Sadyra shared the sleeping space on the floor with her sisters.

"Great! Now look what you've done. We'll never get the little toad back to sleep," Areeza complained.

"Sadie! Sadie! It *is* you!" Sable jumped to her feet; her tiny body draped in a simple shift. "Sleena! Wake up! Sadie's back!"

Sable's tiny feet padded across the dirty floorboards and she jumped into Sadyra's arms, hugging her around the neck; her cornstalk doll clutched tightly in one hand.

Sleena walked into the light to stand beside Sadyra, rubbing at her eyes and smiling up at her big sister.

Sadyra shifted Sable into one arm and hugged Sleena with the other.

Sadyra

"Are you really back?" Sable asked, her absurd question obviously not ridiculous in her eyes.

"Of course, I'm back, silly." Sadyra laughed. "I would never leave you."

Sable's high-pitched, innocent voice sounded sweet in Sadyra's ears. "Dolly and I thought you were kilt."

Sadyra tried not to react. She smiled and removed loose strands of Sable's bangs from in front of her round eyes. "Killed? No. Of course I'm not. You tell Dolly I'm right here." She adjusted her grip. "You're getting to be such a big girl, Sadie's having trouble hanging onto you."

Sable pouted; her trusting eyes regarding Sadyra through long eyelashes.

"Father said the krakens got you." A tear ran down Sable's pudgy cheek.

Sadyra had a hard time not crying with her. She hugged her tight and whispered in her ear. "I'd never let a silly serpent take me away from you and Sleena."

"What about Dolly?"

Sable's pouting lip always filled Sadyra with love. "Not Dolly, either." She kissed Sable's wet cheek and kissed Dolly as well before putting Sable on the floor and turning her sister's shoulders toward their sleeping area. "Now back to bed, you hear? I'll be here in the morning when you wake up."

"You promise?"

"I promise. Now go. Before the trolls get you!" Sadyra gave Sable a playful smack on the bum and nodded at Sleena to do likewise.

Sable screamed and ran, hitting the ground hard and diving under her threadbare blanket.

Sleena didn't move at first. Her intelligent eyes studied Sadyra's face. Without a word, she joined Sable.

Areeza's face was full of malice as she passed Sadyra, but the older woman's features transformed into what Sadyra knew was a fake smile as she handed Gitch a dirty stein full of strong-smelling wine.

"Thank you, ma'am." Gitch nodded and waited for Tural to snatch his tankard from Areeza's shaky hand, before raising it in the air. "To Sadyra."

Tural merely grunted and took a healthy swallow.

Areeza returned with an overflowing stein for herself and gave Sadyra an annoyed look, as if silently asking why Sadyra was still hanging around the table.

Areeza lifted her stein, swallowing several times; making a large dent in its contents. She pulled out one of the rickety stools that her daughters used while at the table and seated herself.

An uncomfortable silence descended over the cabin, accentuating the indecipherable whispers coming from the girls' sleeping area. Sable's wee voice dominated the conversation.

Both of Sadyra's parents cast the dark space a dirty scowl, but thankfully, Gitch spoke up.

"Your daughter is doing quite well in her new position."

Tural glowered over the brim of his stein. "Wrecked any boats yet?"

Sadyra feared Gitch would mention the brawl the previous night, but she needn't have worried.

Tural placed his empty stein in front of Areeza. "Rumour has it she destroyed the *Cauldron*."

Areeza took a long drink to finish her own and got up to fetch another round, clearly not impressed by her husband's attitude. "How 'bout you, captain?"

Gitch shook his head. "Nay. I have to walk home yet. The trail can be tricky in the dark."

Areeza nodded and walked to the back counter beneath the rear window.

Tural turned his dark gaze on Sadyra. "What do you have to say about the *Cauldron*?"

Sadyra

Sadyra swallowed, thankful for Gitch's presence. "I didn't destroy it."

"Ah, but you don't deny you were there?" Tural accepted his refilled stein and drank deeply.

"No but—"

"And you picked a fight with a captain from Thunderhead? A sailor known as Ivar the Blade?"

Sadyra frowned. "I don't know his name."

"So, it *is* true. You did start a fight."

"No. Well, not exactly. He had it coming."

Tural raised his heavy brow. "Did something to you, then, did he?"

"No. Not me. He was getting friendly with Frenza."

"Frenza? The barmaid?"

"Yes. The brute was—"

"What? Enjoying himself after a hard day's work? Ain't your business to be watching out for the *Cauldron* trollop."

"She's my friend."

Tural banged his stein on the table, the noise startling her. "You ain't got time for friends. You're indebted to me and your mother for a new boat." He nodded at Gitch. "You're indebted to the good captain for ruining his main net, and now you're on the hook to refurnish the entire damn bar! What do you expect us to live on if you keep racking up debt?" He pointed his chin at the corner where Sleena and Sable had retired. "Your poor sisters will end up starving one day because of your lackadaisical attitude."

Sadyra felt her ears flush. Her sisters were no doubt listening to their father berate her. She fought the urge to retaliate with harsh words of her own—that the only reason her sisters would starve was because their mother and father spent what little money they had to satisfy their alcohol addiction.

Gitch cleared his throat. "Don't you worry, Mr. and Mrs. Ors. I will see to it that Sadyra is fairly compensated. With the extra hours I intend to have her put in, I'm sure the division of coin can appease all parties."

Tural held the captain's stare. "Humph. She best keep her nose clean, else there soon won't be enough to go around."

Sadyra wanted to scream at her father to get a job of his own, but the only real employer in Fishmonger Bay was either Gitch's crew, or the mercantile. She knew from speaking with Gitch that the captain would never hire her troublemaking father, nor would the tightwad mercantile proprietor, as he only employed family. In the end, she hung her head and muttered, "I will, Father. I promise."

She sensed his glare boring holes into her but she refused to meet his gaze.

Gitch's voice broke the tension. "Sadyra. You've had a couple of hard days. Why don't you retire for the night? I wish to discuss a few things with Tural."

Sadyra sighed. Without a word, she dragged her feet to the back corner, wondering what the captain had to say to her father in private. Removing her belt, she sat on the floor and pulled her boots off; turning her nose up at the sour smell of the ocean.

Sable squeaked with happiness and held the thin blanket up for Sadyra to climb under. Snuggling in close, Sable said softly, "We're glad you ain't kilt, aren't we Dolly?"

Sleena grumbled from where she lay against the log wall. "Go to sleep you little imp. You want Mother to give us all a lickin'?"

Sable hugged Sadyra's arm tight.

Sadyra smiled. There were few times she ever felt truly happy. Lying on the hard floor, beneath a threadbare blanket, sharing body heat with Sable and Sleena was her favourite time of day. She closed her eyes, and ran her fingers through Sable's hair. Reaching over Sable with her other arm, she found Sleena's hand and held it tight.

Though always the aloof one, Sleena returned the squeeze.

Sadyra

One of the Crew

Tramping down the path into Fishmonger Bay the next day, Sadyra shivered in the early morning air. If not for her intrinsic familiarity with the path, she would have missed her step more than she did in the predawn light. She had promised Sable that she would be there in the morning, but had forgotten about attending Gitch's warehouse before sunrise in order to be ready for first light. Exhausted from the previous days, she had no idea what time Gitch had left their cabin. She had fallen asleep almost as soon as she crawled under the blanket.

Not surprising, Gitch was already awake and in his office by the time she entered the warehouse. Half of the crew were there as well with more arriving all the time.

She wasn't sure whether to bother the captain or swallow her trepidation and try assimilating herself into the pre-dawn preparations. Judging by the grumpy faces watching her as she stood inside the exterior door, she decided that perhaps today wasn't the right time to cross that bridge.

The door to the office opened and Scruff's wide beard filled the doorway. Catching her attention, he motioned for her to enter.

Two empty bowls sat on the desk on either side, while a third, full of gruel, rested on the corner of the messy desktop. Scruff motioned with his large eyes that the last bowl was hers. Without a word, he squeezed by her and left the office, banging the door shut behind him.

"Ah, Sadyra." Gitch's crooked-tooth grin pushed aside the apprehension she had experienced while coming here. Not for the first time, she was amazed at how spry the captain always appeared every morning. He was at least twice her age, worked equally hard, and if last night was any indication, slept much less than she did.

He raised his eyebrows as he looked at the untouched bowl. "I don't imagine you've eaten."

Just the sight of the tasteless mush got her salivating. She hadn't had anything to eat since midday, yesterday. Grabbing the bowl, she tore into it, only looking up when the captain opened the door and called out, "Scruff! Another bowl!"

Sitting down again, Gitch said, "I'm sure Slick will be happy to know somebody else likes his slop."

She paused to stare at the captain; swallowing what was in her mouth. "I hope he doesn't know it's for me."

Gitch laughed. "Don't worry. If he spits in it, it can only make it taste better."

Sadyra cringed at the thought, but it didn't deter her from wolfing down the rest of the bowl and the next one Scruff brought in moments later.

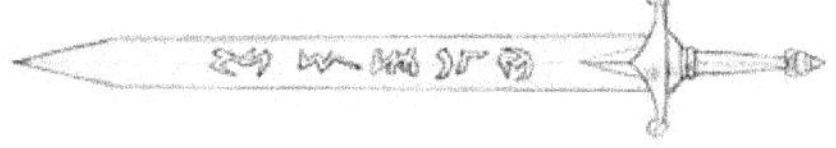

The day's catch netted the crew about the same as yesterday. As they rowed through the gap into the shallower waters fronting Fishmonger Bay, Captain Gitch ordered the boats beached. Ominous clouds were forming on the western horizon; their denseness negating any chance of a beautiful sunset.

Scruff stood in the stern. "Row, runt, row."

Sadyra rowed as hard as she could. Riding the crest of a wave, their dory crunched into the gravel and ground to a halt.

Shipping the oars, she was over the side before either man had time to rise. The captain threw her the bow rope, and jumped down beside her in the shin deep water with a big splash. Together they started to pull the fish and water laden boat up the gravelly incline—their progress halted almost as soon as it began until Scruff leapt over the stern and threw his muscle into it.

Sadyra stumbled as one of her boots sunk into the wet stones and just missed being run over by the boat. The near brush with what could have proven very painful, if not seriously injuring her, made her snap, "Hey! Easy, fuzz face. You trying to kill me?"

Scruff poked his head around the rear of the boat. "Ain't got all day, runt. Tide'll be pulling out soon and the sun's about to set."

The crews beaching the boats close by laughed as they passed them, dragging their boats onto dry land. Slim's voice sounded over the waves and crunching stone, "Dames and giants. What a pair you got, Cap!"

Sadyra didn't dignify either man with a rebuttal. Grabbing the rope between Gitch and the boat, she hauled on it with everything she had.

The next hour went by in a flurry of activity. Boats were emptied of their catch; heavy buckets brimming with fish were lugged into the warehouse to an awaiting group of older townsfolk—mostly women—who earnestly began filleting the catch and preparing them for the mercantile.

Sadyra noticed a larger boat tied to the jetty, near the shore. Toiling alongside the bare-chested crew, she took a chance and asked one of them, "Who's boat?"

A red-headed sailor, sporting a well-trimmed beard, considered her for a moment as they trudged toward the warehouse with buckets in hand. "Cap's called in a favour from the Head. Need a sleek boat to get the surplus to the city market now that the ship is wrecked."

Sadyra looked out to sea, studying the brooding stormfront. "And who's going to do that?"

The man shrugged. "Whoever Cap decides." He took a few more steps and added, "Judging by the weather coming in, I'm thinking he and Scruff'll likely take it themselves. Cap ain't likely to risk anyone else."

The sailor tromped on ahead and through the propped open door.

Although the increasing breeze off the ocean and the waning sun dropping behind grey clouds on the horizon had dropped the temperature considerably, sweat streamed from Sadyra's face and glistened on her exposed arms—smearing the day's grime with unsightly streaks.

The crew worked with dogged determination to get their chores done—often bumping into one another and cussing. To Sadyra's bizarre pleasure, she wasn't excluded. Twice someone rammed into her, knocking her off stride. The second time, she dropped to a knee in the unforgiving gravel; struggling not to upset her bucket.

"Watch it, runt." A blonde-haired young man, not much older than herself, complained. "Get out of the way if you can't keep up."

She glowered at Frenza's brother, Jenza. She used to have a crush on him when they were growing up. Jenza was three years older than Frenza and had never had any time for his sister's immature friends.

She unsteadily got her second leg under her and hustled after him, staring at the ponytail dangling between his muscular shoulders. "I was just slowing down so you could keep up."

Jenza stepped onto the wooden walkway abutting the rear of the warehouse and looked at her hot on his heels.

She nodded. "Ya. I thought it was Frenza following me."

He looked at her like he had just stepped in a fresh pile of troll dung. Without another word, he stomped into the warehouse, delivered his buckets, and shouldered past her to gather his next load.

She dropped her buckets, amazed she had actually carried them that far without putting them down except for when Jenza had knocked her aside. Smiling, she followed Jenza into the twilight. Her attempt at speaking to another member of the crew as an equal hadn't gone over as well as she had hoped.

The ocean breeze increased to strong gusts by the time Sadyra and the rest of the crew had finished cleaning and mending their nets and were carrying them toward the warehouse.

As she had done the night before, she struggled with the huge net; its bulk heavy and unwieldy.

Scruff stomped up beside her bearing a similar net, carrying the burden as if it were a small blanket. "Want me to take that for you, runt, before you hurt yourself?"

There was nothing more in the whole world that she wanted at that moment. She looked around and noticed several other beleaguered faces of the crew watching her interaction with Scruff as they made their way across the tough footing of the loose gravel underfoot.

She stepped sideways to create distance between herself and Scruff. Making sure her voice carried, she said, "Pfft. As if. Carry your own net and mind your own business."

Her response raised several eyebrows.

Scruff glared at her.

She stumbled toward him, turning an ankle, and fell to her knees, spilling her net on the beach.

A chorus of roars went up around her.

Scruff stopped long enough to shake his head and followed his laughing companions into the warehouse.

Spitting with embarrassment-fueled anger, she gathered the net in a heap and charged after the others, tripping on the edges dragging along the beach. Once on the wooden walkway, a loop of netting caught itself on the end of a plank and ripped it out of her hands. She screamed in frustration. Balling up the net, she wrestled its unwieldy mass through the door and into the warehouse.

Slim approached, halfway to where they stowed the nets for the night in the hanging room—a large open space; its walls riddled with long stakes driven into the wall. He paused, eyeing the mass of unkempt netting she struggled with. "Trouble with your net?"

She glared at the massive redhead; biting back unpleasant words that came to mind.

He nodded at the rope spilling over her arms. "How do you expect to hang it up like that?"

Not caring about the repercussions, she shored up what little strength remained in her arms and chucked the pile of wet rope at him.

As big as he was, he wasn't prepared to suddenly catch the cumbersome pile. He flailed his arms and stumbled backward. His foot entangled in a loop and down he went—the bulk of the net covering him from head to toe.

Sadyra stood over him and pointed a finger in his face. "If you're so smart, figure it out yourself."

A chorus of laughter and whistles thundered throughout the warehouse from sailors and packers alike.

The shade of Slim's face turned redder than his beard as he flailed about beneath the netting, entangling himself further—all the while turning the air blue with words Sadyra had rarely heard spoken.

Her anger drained from her as the gravity of what she had done settled in.

Captain Gitch stormed out of the office. "What's going on?" He assessed the situation, nodding with his chin in one hand.

Sadyra was pretty sure the captain struggled to keep from laughing.

The way he spoke confirmed her suspicion. "I suggest you get yourself as far away from here as fast as you can. Once he figures out how to extricate himself, I'm thinking you won't want to be anywhere near."

Sadyra wasted no time exiting the warehouse and scrambling across the commons. Other than the fact that she would get to spend time with her sisters, there weren't many occasions that she looked forward to going home. Tonight was one of them.

The following days turned into weeks. As each day passed, Sadyra made the trip down the steep hill into Fishmonger Bay before sunrise; rarely making it back home before the sun set. Nothing came of her run in with Slim but the crew made sure it wasn't forgotten. Nor were her antics in the *Cauldron*, or the day she had pitched Scruff overboard.

Ever so slowly, most of the crew accepted her into their fold. Slick had apologized to her in private one afternoon north of the Summoning Stone as they went ashore to rest and eat. She wasn't sure when it had actually happened, but as the summer solstice approached, she actually felt like she was one of the lads.

During periods of inhospitable weather, she had enlisted men like Slim, Slick, and Jenza to teach her how to fight with her hands and a knife. Her fiery temper and fierce determination helped her become a quick learner. Many nights she returned home unable to count the number of bruises and abrasions she had received as a reward for her efforts.

On the days that Captain Gitch allowed the crew to return early, Scruff had made it a point to teach her how to use her bow more efficiently; setting up a wide assortment of archery butts upon the beach beyond the fleet of overturned dories. Many of the crew would participate in a friendly competition to see who was the best marksman—after Scruff. Sadyra enjoyed these days and her skills improved remarkably over time.

One sweltering evening, while being attended by the healer, Henga, for a nasty contusion she picked up sparring with Jenza, Captain Gitch ruffled her hair and asked, “How’s it feel to be one of the crew?”

As happy as that proclamation made her, not everything about being a part of the crew sat well with her. A few times she had been forced to politely decline one of the lad’s advances on her as a woman. Her reputation as someone who shouldn’t be trifled with prevented them from pushing their intentions beyond the inquiry stage.

The sailors weren’t the only ones who had come to appreciate her pretty face and generally cheery attitude. On more than one occasion she had caught Bano watching her from afar as she joked and wrested with the members of the crew. Whenever he realized she was aware of him, Bano would storm away. She didn’t miss his dull, brown stare over the last few months, but every time she saw him, it reminded her of the future her parents had set out for her.

The imminent arrival of the summer solstice served to drive that fact home. It signified that there was only half a year remaining until the Mating Festival. Given her parents’ desire to see her married off, the spring equinox promised to be the worst one yet.

Sadyra

If Only

As the hot summer months waned toward autumn, Captain Gitch decided the crew deserved to take half a day off to enjoy one of the last few days of unusually good weather the region had been experiencing.

Sadyra folded their net and stomped across the gravel toward the warehouse, but Scruff uncharacteristically relieved her of the burden. He nodded toward the hill where her family cabin sat hidden behind the brush. "Fetch your hunting gear and meet me on the moors this side of the canyon."

Sadyra gawked as he tromped away; the heavy net barely causing his muscular arms to flex.

"Don't keep me waiting," he added without turning around.

Raising her eyebrows, she considered his retreating form. A small smile crept up her face and she raced across the commons to attack the steep hill north of Fishmonger Bay.

Areeza and her sisters stared after her as she burst into their cabin, stole to the back corner and changed her clothes. Collecting her gear, she smiled at Sleena and ruffled Sable's hair; not bothering to give her mother the time of day.

Before anyone could question her, she scrambled down the path toward the main trail; hastily pulling her thin cloth and leather vambraces over her forearms—a dozen arrows rattling around in the quiver slung over her shoulder. Her archery gear and the clothing she chose to wear while hunting were her valued possessions. She took great care to keep them in good condition.

By the time the edge of the canyon came into view, she thought she might faint due to lack of food, but she needn't have worried. She located Scruff by following the smell of a small cookfire.

"Whatcha cooking?" she asked, walking up to the fire. Her question was meant as more of a casual conversation starter than to inquire about Scruff's preparations. The all too familiar aroma of fish, more than enough to answer her question.

"Fish. What else?"

She laughed nervously. "Of course."

Though Scruff had never given her the inkling that his intentions toward her were anything but as one colleague to another, being alone with him this far away from the village left her mind swirling with a peculiar sensation—one that took her outside of her comfort zone. If she allowed herself to dwell on it, the thoughts whirling around her head filled her with the fanciful notion that this was how she ought to feel in the presence of Bano, her fiancé.

She turned away from Scruff's gaze and swallowed. Shaking her head, she shrugged free of her gear and found a rock to sit on across the fire. "There'd better be enough for two, or you're gonna starve."

Scruff's intense stare left her thinking that perhaps her attempt at humour had fallen on deaf ears, but a subtle nod and a faint smirk informed her that it hadn't.

"There's enough for both of us," was all he said.

Sadyra forced a smile and broke eye contact.

Their mid-afternoon meal out of the way, and the fire extinguished, Scruff led her onto a flat section of forested area dominating the western lip of a deep ravine. He stopped atop a large shelf of rock that commanded a breathtaking view of the coastal region far below. White-capped waves rolled northward toward Fishmonger Bay—the temple rooftop barely visible to the right of where they stood.

Scruff surprised her by grabbing a handful of her waist-length hair and ran it through his rough fingers.

Not trusting herself to speak, and with nowhere to retreat to without falling over the lip of the outcrop, she stared at his hand; oddly moved by the tenderness of his touch. She dared to look him in the eye and swallowed. The softness in his gaze took her breath away.

Scruff swallowed deeply as a touch of colour tinged the exposed skin on his cheeks. He let her hair slip through his fingers. "You really should consider cutting it."

His comment threw her. "Cut my hair?"

Fiery intensity replaced the tenderness in his eyes. "Aye. It wouldn't do to get it caught in your bowstring." He stepped beside her and looked out to sea. "Nor would it be advantageous in a fight. Gives your opponent something with which to inflict pain."

She gaped. "I'm a fisherwoman. In a backwater village. Other than an occasional bar fight," she noticed a slight upturn to his lips, "why would I ever have to worry about an opponent?"

Scruff shrugged.

When he returned her gaze, she instinctively knew what he was thinking about. Her father. She sighed. If Scruff only knew how terrified she was of her father, he'd know there was no way she would ever be able to defend herself against the despicable brute.

Time stood still. Gusts of wind blew off the ocean, wafting through their hair as they stood exposed upon the jag of rock. Clad in a sleeveless, grey suede and leather top, and padded leather breeches that disappeared into knee-high boots, Sadyra shivered.

"Come. Let's get started." Scruff jumped off the backside of the outcrop and started away. "The sun is setting earlier each day. It won't due to be caught up here after dark."

Sadyra

It was with a bizarre sadness that Sadyra followed the gruff man from the rock ledge—as if something magical had happened in that moment, frozen in time. Something she had been immediately frightened of, but now that the moment had passed, she was afraid it might never happen again.

Scruff stopped at the head of a path that led down into the canyon. "Today, I'm going to teach you a couple of subtle tricks that will help you track someone."

She frowned. "Who would I ever need to track?"

He shrugged. "Fair enough. How about a deer, then?"

That made more sense.

"I also want to work on your archery skills. You've become quite adept at hitting stationary targets, its time you learned how to shoot a target while you *and* it are moving."

"Sounds good." She nodded, finding it hard to look him in the eye without fear of becoming tongue-tied or having her cheeks flame red.

"Alright. Once I show you, I'm going to forge ahead and try to remain hidden. If you are able to follow my trail, you'll come across targets blowing in the trees. I want you to shoot them as you move. Make sense?"

Sadyra nodded, not trusting herself to speak; fearing she might say something silly. A giddy feeling bubbled in her stomach. She could tell he felt uncomfortable looking at her as well.

It was hard to concentrate on his words as she snatched quick looks at his profile and admired his rugged hands. It was all she could do not to reach out and grab onto his arm as he stood up, to keep him from moving away from her.

After he had explained the ways to identify the passage of an animal by observing subtle differences in the foliage and other indicators of a creature's passing, he told her to remain where she was until the shadow of a stick he placed in the dirt at their feet touched a line he had drawn.

Watching his broad shoulders disappear into the heather, she admonished herself for her foolishness. She had read something into their brief encounter on the rock ledge that was obviously absurd. She sighed and sat on the ground, staring at the stick—her mind wandering to places it had never gone before.

She gasped as she realized the shadow cast by the stick had passed the mark Scruff had drawn on the ground. Lost in fanciful notions of a different life, she had forgotten to keep an eye on the passage of time.

She stood and looked around. The sun was dropping over the ocean but it would be a long time before she had to worry about darkness falling over the land.

At first, it was easy to follow Scruff's path. She had seen him go. Locating the tell-tale signs of his passage, though not blatantly apparent, with closer examination, she realized with a sense of wonder that she was able to follow his path throughout the wilderness. Targets of wood swaying from low-lying branches, identifiable by strips of cloth tied to them, confirmed that she was getting the knack of tracking.

Running across the mountainside and shooting arrows at the targets Scruff had set out—presumably before she had arrived—exhilaration fueled her desire to prove herself to the mysterious man. She was quite pleased and a little surprised at her proficiency with her bow. Most of the arrows had hit their intended targets.

She stopped at each target to retrieve her arrows—oft times having to climb the tree or outcropping in order to dislodge them. Of the targets she missed, she wasted a lot of time searching for the errant arrows; often having to force herself to consider them lost.

As the afternoon wore on, she came across a steep path dropping into the canyon. Bending low to inspect the ground and examine the foliage, she was at a loss as to where he had gone. With the sun sinking toward the horizon and its earlier warmth fading, she felt relatively confident that Scruff wouldn't have ventured into the canyon.

If she didn't find him soon, however, they would run the risk of not making it back to Fishmonger Bay before nightfall. The mountain slopes weren't the best place to be after the sundown.

Her gaze took in the endless terrain of trees, rock, and the ever-present canyon marring the mountainside. She could almost feel the eyes of hungry trolls.

Besides her parents—her father in particular—not much scared Sadyra, but the thought of braving the mountainside when darkness fell made her heart race. If she didn't find Scruff soon, she'd have to decide whether or not to leave him to fend for himself. She pitied any troll who chose to tangle with the man.

She backtracked until she located the last sign of his passage, but couldn't find anything that even remotely indicated where he had gone from there.

Fretting she needed to make a difficult decision, she absently noticed her cramping stomach. The midafternoon meal hadn't been enough to sustain her through all of the running around. She walked back to the junction, scanning the ground on either side, but couldn't locate anything.

Scruff couldn't have just disappeared. He had either kept on along the brink of the canyon, or slipped down the steep trail, perhaps cutting back on their previous position to sneak up on her.

She contemplated returning to where they began, half expecting to find him there. But, if she was wrong, she would throw away any chance of locating him before nightfall. The last thing she wanted was to be a disappointment in his eyes.

Frustrated, she resisted the urge to throw something. Her intuition told her she needed to descend to the canyon floor, but common sense told her that would risk becoming hopelessly lost in the ensuing darkness.

Left with little choice, she thought about accepting defeat and making her way back to the main trail home. It was time she stopped fooling herself. She wasn't a tracker. Scruff's instruction had been informative, and certainly a good first step in learning how to locate the clues that only trackers knew how to unearth, but she wasn't about to fool herself into thinking she was anywhere close to mastering the feat.

A howl split the ironic tranquility of the mountainside, setting her nerves on end. The wolf's cry left her struggling to contain her fear. Irrational or not, she was powerless to prevent it from dominating her thoughts. Behind every thick tree trunk, inside every shadowy crevice of rock, she envisioned an eight-foot, hairy beast with bloodshot eyes and yellowed fangs. Watching. Waiting.

The howl sounded like it had come from farther up the path she followed. If Scruff *had* gone that way, she doubted the wolf would have made a noise. Swallowing her misgivings, that likely meant he had ventured into the canyon. With every bit of courage she could muster, she started down the steep slope—her soft-soled boots slipping on the loose scree.

At the base of the trail, she searched the cliffs on either side; much of the canyon floor lost in the creeping shadows of approaching night. Her gravity induced flight down the trail from above hadn't allowed her to inspect the path for signs of Scruff. Looking up the narrow trail, her own passage had erased any sign he might have left.

With nothing to go on, she started south along the rubble-strewn canyon floor; scanning the desolate terrain. At some point, she would have to come across the path that led out of the canyon; a part of the main trail ascending from Fishmonger Bay and continuing on to the old cabin near the summit of Peril's Peak.

Shadows deepened and a cool wind blew down the length of the defile. Sadyra stopped to gather her bearings. She had been in the canyon a few times over the years, but she had a sinking feeling that she had never been this far south. The unremarkable terrain blended into itself, providing little in the way of landmarks with which to gauge her location.

If she wasn't mistaken, she should have come across the main trail up to the rim a while ago. Nor had she seen any sign that Scruff had been in the canyon at all. The ground consisted mostly of stone, rather than dirt and plant life. Even if he had come this way, she would never be able to track his movements with her limited skills.

It was hard to see beyond several feet in any direction. Night sounds that were familiar while lying under her blankets at home seemed scarier now that she was beneath an open sky, alone.

"Scruff…?" she called out half-heartedly.

Shaking her head at her foolish decision to enter the canyon, she raised her voice. "Scruff!"

His name echoed off the canyon walls, slowly dissipating into the night. As the echoes faded, she looked around in fear, mumbling, "That's great, Sadyra. Let everything that wants to eat you know where you're at."

Pulling her waterskin over her shoulder, she grimaced—its contents were almost gone. It promised to be a long night.

A deep throated growl from somewhere above made her hunker down and search the dark walls looming overhead. A growl she knew well. Living atop the hill overlooking Fishmonger Bay, she recalled the times her father had sat in the middle of their cabin with a bow strung on his lap, prepared to defend them should a troll attempt to enter their hut. Though she had never seen a live one, the image of the dead trolls the villagers had killed defending their homes was a sight she would never forget.

She found it hard to keep an arrow nocked with her hands shaking—more from fright than the dropping temperature. Fearful she had missed the trail to the top, she decided the only choice left to her was to backtrack and search for the path she had come down.

Another growl caused her to stop walking and hide behind a large boulder—eyes wide with fear. Hunkered beside the rock, she swallowed and scanned the dark wall at her back. Trolls were rumoured to have excellent night vision and were able to climb like spiders.

She stepped away from the boulder. Cowering against the canyon wall was probably the worst thing she could do. She knew she should keep moving but couldn't generate the nerve.

The night crawled by. A full moon crested the eastern rim of the canyon, shedding light on her surroundings. Thankful at first, she quickly realized she disliked the shadows the moonlight created—her mind rife with things that weren't there. She gulped. Or were they?

Unfamiliar noises sent her heart racing. Skittering and buzzing, hissing and crying sounds had her looking every which way at once, expecting the worst.

As the moon's path took it beyond the western rim, a growl rumbled from down the canyon floor. It came again a short while later. Closer.

Without having to think about it, her feet started moving—slowly at first, but as she stared over her shoulder, her pace picked up—the rubble-strewn ground tripping her as she staggered along its uneven surface.

A deeper growl sounded directly above her from somewhere along the western wall. She froze and searched the cliff, its face shrouded in darkness. She couldn't see a thing, but a cascade of rock debris made her cry out in alarm.

Not caring how many times she stumbled on the uncertain terrain, she careened up the canyon, desperately seeking a way out.

A more urgent growl rose up behind her as something landed in the darkness against the base of the cliff.

Finding it difficult to breathe, Sadyra sprinted up the canyon faster than her feet had ever carried her—the remaining arrows in her quiver rattling loudly in the relative quiet. Above the clatter, a rapid cadence of what could only be claws clicking on stone followed her.

Boots sliding on the ground, she almost ran past the trail leading up to the western rim. She hazarded a look down the canyon. Had her fear not constricted her throat, she would have screamed at the unnerving apparition charging at her.

Easily eight-feet tall and covered in long black fur from head to toe, a gangly troll lurched toward her—the intensity in its eyes caused the fine hair on her arms to stand on end.

Attacking the uncertain path leading up to the top, her thighs screamed at her long before she was halfway, but the adrenaline coursing through her veins kept her feet digging.

She slipped and fell to a knee several times before cresting the western rim of the canyon. Not waiting to determine if the troll had closed the distance on her, she bolted south along the canyon's rim, conscious to keep the dark cleft far enough to the left to avoid falling over its brink.

Thoughts of Scruff assaulted her as she ran. Where was he? Had he left her to fend for herself? Or had he…?

Her eyes welled up, blurring the shadowy landscape. Fueled by terror and a wild imagination, she envisioned Scruff lying somewhere in the darkness, bleeding to death. She hadn't paid enough attention to his tracking lessons and had failed him.

The perpetual crash of the ocean broke on the shore, unseen far below. She didn't think she was up to running the entire way back to the village. Not daring to look back, she searched for the six thick trees that were clustered together on the rim of the canyon, their trunks forming what had always seemed to her as a tunnel. They marked the end of the path that would take her to the shoreline trail south of Fishmonger Bay.

A mist rose up from the ground obscuring the terrain further; the full moon cast the mountainside in an ethereal glow. Daring to hope she had lost the beast, she looked over

her shoulder and stumbled. The troll gained on her at an alarming rate.

Trying desperately to keep from falling, she careened toward the canyon's edge; crashing through the underbrush as it tugged at her and attempted to snag her feet.

Twigs snapped and small rocks spilled over the lip of the canyon as the troll lumbered after her, his progress not impeded by the way the brush held up Sadyra.

She contemplated throwing herself over the edge. Either she would land on something below or the fall would kill her. A quick death would be preferable to being mauled by a troll. Searching for a spot that might provide her a chance of surviving the fall, she realized the cluster of trees she had been searching for rose up before her.

Another scenario formed in her mind.

Rounding the edge of the tree closest to the brink, she grasped its rough surface to keep from sliding off of its exposed roots and falling over the edge of the canyon. It took all of the nerve she had and a little more she didn't know she possessed to remain there. She had to make sure the troll kept along the edge of the canyon if her plan were to have any chance of working.

She fought to steady her breathing. It would be close.

The greasy fur matting the trolls hideous face glinted in the moonlight—its veined eyes, wild with fury.

Sadyra took several quick steps into the tunnel formed by the tree trunks. They grew so close together that they formed a solid wall of bark on either side.

Steeling her nerves, she had one chance.

She shrugged her bow free and gripped it—harder than she had been trained to. Taking a deep breath, her nerves jumped with every snap of a fallen branch the troll's progress precipitated.

A throaty growl pierced the night, shaking her resolve and echoing off the heights beyond the canyon's far rim.

Sadyra

A branch above Sadyra's head creaked and trembled. Cowering, she held her hands over her head, and tried to still her hammering heart as a raven took flight.

Swallowing her fear, she straightened and faced the tunnel to where she knew the troll would come.

Sadyra

She fought to keep her hands from trembling. She would only get one shot.

Claws crunched into the bark. A massive black paw rounded the last tree trunk growing up from the canyon's edge. A black foot, closely resembling a human's but covered in black fur and tipped with curved claws, dug into the roots upon which it stood.

The troll's head appeared in the gap, its watery eyes finding hers. It opened its mouth and bellowed so loud, her nocked arrow nearly slipped from the string. Jumping into the space between the trees, it raised padded forepaws and came at her; hooked claws extended.

Her bow shook as she pulled the string taut with her left hand—the arrowhead rattled against the bow, threatening to fall off her white-knuckled finger. Closing her eyes tight, she let it fly.

The arrow flew true, taking the troll at the base of the neck. Face contorted in pain, the troll stumbled backward, grasping at the arrow with its forepaws. A horrific screech escaped its black lips as the arrow ripped free. It stopped staggering toward the brink of the yawning canyon and roared at the sky.

Shocked that her arrow hadn't taken the troll down, Sadyra stepped backward, shaking her head. She pulled another from her quiver but her hands trembled so hard she couldn't notch it—eyes rivetted on the nightmare coming at her between the trees.

A twig snapped behind her. Before she had a chance to react, a large body charged past.

Scruff dropped his shoulder, smashing into the troll—his momentum lifted the startled creature's feet from the ground and impelled it through the air.

The troll's gangly arms waved in the air in a futile attempt to stop its flight over the canyon's lip. A guttural roar echoed across the mountainside as it fell to it death.

Sadyra

Scruff dropped to his knees, nearly following the troll. Catching himself, he shot back to his feet and ran to Sadyra. "Are you okay?"

Sadyra stared at him, shaking so hard she couldn't talk. She nodded her head, the motion barely visible; her terror-filled eyes on the spot the troll had just occupied.

Scruff wrapped his arms around her. "It's okay. It's gone. We killed it."

Sadyra nodded into his chest. Her mind numb, she derived comfort from Scruff's touch.

Scruff broke the embrace and grasped her by the shoulders to hold her at arms' length. A big smile parted his unruly beard—happiness and pride in his eyes. "You faced down a troll. And won!"

She swallowed, her wide-eyed gaze holding his, and nodded ever so slightly.

He rubbed her bare arms. "Come on. You're trembling. Let's get you off the mountain before the rest of the trolls take an interest in us."

Sadyra

The Reckoning

The days following Sadyra's incident with the troll passed by in a blur. Still roiling from her brush with a gruesome death, she struggled to come to terms with what had happened between her and Scruff. Though pleasant in her company, he seemed like a different person. He kept to himself more now than he ever had.

The butterflies in her stomach while in his company never ceased to flutter, but Scruff's aloofness had her questioning if they had shared an intimate moment at all. She struggled to accept the fact that she was likely mistaken.

Bringing home a decent wage had appeased her parents somewhat at first, but her father never let her forget that besides providing for her family, her biggest concern should be the acquisition of another fishing boat. Even though she was sure she was providing her parents a better life than they had known while eking out a living for themselves, the nearer the equinox approached, the darker their mood became.

Eight days before the summer solstice, her father's blackening mood boiled over. It had been months since the day he had chased her into the ocean. From that point on, he had never laid another hand on her, though there were a few times recently that made Sadyra fear the return of his usual ways. As much as her father's blind rages terrified her, she no longer dreaded taking a beating. He had a big surprise coming if, and when, he dared to lay a hand on her or her sisters again.

Sadyra

Sitting at the dinner table, Tural threw back the contents of his stein and slammed it on the battered wood, making everybody jump. His brooding stare bore into Sadyra. "You. Come with me."

Sadyra gulped. She looked questioningly around the table at the scared faces of her sisters and the ever-present scowl that twisted her mother's features.

She couldn't recall doing anything wrong. In fact, she was waiting until after their scant supper to share exciting news with everyone—her father in particular.

Ensuring her knife sat firmly sheathed at her waist, she pushed her lopsided stool back and followed Tural through the door and into the darkness; making a point to keep her distance.

With unsteady steps, Tural led her around the back of the hut and halfway across the sloped clearing beyond that rose to merge with a trail traversing the mountainside. The path climbed steeply southward, accessing the steep slopes beneath Peril's Peak, and meandered northward toward a great valley two hard days walk away. The valley of the dragons.

He turned; his face barely visible beneath a moonless sky. "Bano tells me you haven't been paying attention to him."

Sadyra rolled her eyes. "So?"

The way Tural adjusted his stance told her that his temper was rising. She had seen it too many times not to recognize the danger.

"So?" Tural took a step toward her. "You're betrothed. The Shell's have promised a fair dowry for your hand. Don't mess this up or…"

She waited for him to finish his thought, but he turned to face the dark hulk of the mountain towering behind them.

"I don't love Bano."

His evil glare snapped back to her. "What do you know of love? Traipsing about with Gitch's men has filled your head with fanciful delusions."

Sadyra frowned. "That's not true. I may be young, but I know how I feel."

"Ya? Well, let me tell you something, little miss know-it-all. Your idea of love is skewed by false hope. You're immature. Fooled by lust. Relationships are built. Look at me and your mother. It's taken many years to get to where we're at."

Sadyra gaped. A relationship like her parents was the last type she wished for.

Considering his statement, she hazarded a glance at their rundown cabin. It would be a miracle if it survived the coming winter. She and her sisters wore hand-me-down, ill-fitting clothing—ripped and worn more than they were in good repair. Until recently, they had struggled to eat well on a regular basis. She had no idea what lay at the root of her parents' relationship, but love was the last thing she would attribute to the way they treated each other.

Nor did she feel sorry for them. From what she could tell, her mother and father were victims of their own making. The older Sadyra became, the more she believed they drank themselves into submission to avoid something they were unwilling to deal with. With regard to love, she had never seen them share a kiss or hold hands, let alone speak endearing words to one another.

It was all she could do to bite her tongue. Something lay at the root of her parents' troubles. Something so dark and sinister that they had resorted to the numbing effect alcohol provided to ease them through the day. She had suspected this for years, but broaching the subject only made matters worse. Whatever the cause of their angst, it was up to them to come to terms with it—not take it out on their children. Her and Sable especially.

A conversation she had had with Bano the day after she had damaged the family boat made its way to the forefront of her thoughts. He had questioned her about her heritage. A topic he had taken a peculiar interest in.

Sadyra

Standing on the hilltop at the end of the path leading from their cabin, Bano had asked, *'And he hasn't said anything more to you about your ancestors?'*

Later that same day, Bano had mentioned the grave markers at the end of the path and asked if she ever wondered about who they were.

For as long as she could recall, Bano had been curious about things she cared little for. He liked to point out that the dilapidated hut she lived in had been in her family for over five hundred years. Looking at it now, it was a wonder no one had torn it down long ago.

Ever since that discussion with Bano, one of his proclamations had struck a chord and remained with her—surfacing during the dark hours in the middle of the night; keeping her awake as she stared into the shadows of the hut looking for something that felt just out of sight; *'A witch used to live in your cabin. A family of them...That means you're related to the Dragon Witch.'*

"Are you listening?"

Tural's angered tone snapped her out of her reverie. She blinked several times. She had no idea what he had been on about, nor did she care. Instead, a question escaped her lips before she had a chance to think better of it. "Are we really related to the Dragon Witch?"

Tural's face looked as if someone had slapped it hard. "Huh?"

Sadyra cringed. The last time she had brought it up, Tural had reacted so badly, it had almost cost Sadyra her life.

Her hand went to her knife handle just in case. "Bano claims we're descended from witches. Is that true?"

Tural stuttered, the sounds he made making no sense. And then he was on her; powerful hands gripping Sadyra's shoulder so hard she cried out. He put his face into hers; his breath rank with poor hygiene and stale ale. "So, it's Bano putting these ideas into your head, is it?"

She nodded faintly, afraid to speak lest she infuriate him further—all sense of her earlier bravado about facing her father had evaporated with the night's mist.

"You tell that whelp to mind his own bloody business, you hear?"

On the verge of tears, Sadyra swallowed and nodded again.

"I'll thrash his scrawny hide the next time I lay eyes on the twerp. Teach him what happens to people who go about spreading nasty rumours."

He shoved her so hard she stumbled and fell to her backside.

She was on her feet at once, scrambling toward the cabin. Shocked she had dragged Bano into this, she shook her head—partly dreading what her father might do to Bano, but mostly because she knew what was about to happen to her. "Father, no."

Tural advanced, swaying from side to side in his drunken state. "Don't you dare run from me."

Unable to keep her mouth shut, she yelled through her fear, "Or what? You'll hit me?"

She thought of her knife but wasn't brave enough to bare steel in her father's presence again. She staggered sideways, her frightened gaze switching back and forth between the side of the cabin and the demon who claimed to be her father.

Tural tripped on his own feet and stopped; shoulders swaying as he pointed. "Get back here right now. Your mother wanted to wait until the Mating Festival, but you've forced my hand. It's time we faced the reckoning."

Sadyra shook her head; the image of her enraged father blurred through a veil of tears. Today was supposed to be a happy one. A day that she had actually looked forward to coming home for the first time in as long as she could remember. To see the proud look on her parents' faces when she informed them she had purchased a new, family boat. Well, not new exactly, but new to her.

With Captain Gitch's blessing, she had taken a smaller dory down to Thunderhead yesterday and purchased the boat from the North Shore Fishery—the same fishery her father did business with. Skipper had assured her that with a little tender, loving care, they could make it seaworthy again.

Swab and Skipper had brought it up the coast, and were waiting for her when she had rowed Gitch and Scruff into Fishmonger Bay this afternoon. On top of the bountiful catch, seeing the beaming face of Swab proudly watching her come in; his dirty blonde hair blowing about as he stood on the jetty above a small dory, had been a glorious sight. Skipper claimed Swab had worked all night to get it ready.

"Are you deaf?" Tural took an unsteady step and caught himself before he fell sideways. "Don't make this worse on yourself or I'll throw your scraps to the krakens."

His cruel words stung. Not that she hadn't heard them before, but because she knew in her heart, as much as she had convinced herself she was capable of standing up to the tyrant, she would never have the nerve.

She surprised herself and hissed, but that was the extent of her ability to fight back. The ludicrousness of the situation infuriated her. She had stood up to Slim, and had fought Slick without a second thought, but the idea of facing off against her father terrified her.

Fighting through paralyzing fear, she took another step away from him. And then another.

He called after her, but with each irate word flung her way, her legs moved faster. The last thing she heard him say got her feet running.

"If I ever see your sorry face around here again, I'll cut it from your skull and feed it to you." His voice rose to a maniacal scream, "You hear me, witch!"

The cabin disappeared behind her as she bolted down the path to the main trail. Not stopping at the juncture, she scrambled down the steep hillside leading into Fishmonger

Bay—falling twice and scraping her knees, elbows, and palms, but she didn't feel the pain.

Sadyra

Tougher than Life

Moonlight filtered through a break in the clouds, its full face reflecting off the unusually still waters of the reef-infested bay fronting Captain Gitch's warehouse.

Cowering beneath a discarded net Swab had mended and included for her as a gift, Sadyra waited out the night in the scuppers of her little dory, unable to get her father's last words from her head.

'You hear me, witch!' Repeated itself over and over. Each time sending shivers through her.

As the night deepened, she was occasionally jarred from the immobilizing terror by the tell-tale crunch of someone walking across the beach. Her immediate fear was that her father had found her, but whoever it was, they never stepped onto the jetty.

Fleeing into Fishmonger Bay, her first thought was to seek out the captain, but shame prevented her from asking him for help. She had striven so hard to become one of the crew, she was afraid that her weakness in the face of her father's rage would demean her in the lads' eyes.

She had no idea how long she laid in the boat trembling; scared of what the future had in store. She had abandoned her sisters. Again. She clung to the hope that they weren't in any real danger. Sable was too young, and Sleena, for whatever reason, seemed exempt from the blame their parents saddled her and Sable with.

Deep down, she wanted to charge up the hill and extricate her sisters from harm's way. She could envision herself doing so, but to actually face the wrath of her father was too much to bear.

The familiar squeal of the warehouse door pierced the night—its sudden noise jerking her body with a spasm of fright. The sound of footsteps on the dock planks made her hunker down lower.

The steps approached, slow and steady—stopping before they reached her boat. She fretted that her boat was the only one still tied to the pier. The captain had ordered the fishing fleet beached based on Slick's prediction that a stormfront would hit the bay area before morning.

An eerie silence settled over the water. The soft lap of the ocean swells spilling on the gravel beach the only sound louder than her hammering heart. She willed the person to move on, but whoever it was had either vanished into thin air or was being unnaturally still.

She fingered her knife hilt. It had to be someone from the crew—or perhaps one of the warehouse workers. Judging by the position of the moon, she doubted anyone would still be left in the warehouse. Except maybe the captain and Scruff.

The thought of seeing Gitch's tough mug, complete with his long, broken nose and balding head, helped ease her crushing anxiety at being found out.

As quietly as possible, she lifted her head enough to peer over the edge of the dory and the dock beyond. The sight staring back at her snatched her breath away.

Scruff's large brown eyes bore into her; his unruly beard glistening in the moonlight and shrouding his face.

"You gonna stay there all night?"

Even though she knew he had seen her, his voice jarred her nerves. She swallowed and forced a smile. "Thinking about it."

Scruff raised his eyebrows. "Suit yourself. Ain't likely a troll will find you out here. They don't like water much."

He grunted and turned on his heels to strut down the jetty without looking back. "Kind of like dwarfs in that regard."

Sadyra

The hinges of the warehouse door pierced the night, flooding the immediate area around him with light, and then he was gone.

Puzzled, she was convinced his presence on the dock hadn't been a coincidence. How he had known she was there raised many questions. The fact that he might have seen her sneak across the beach and pad softly along the jetty made the most sense, but she didn't believe that was the case. There was something mysterious about Gitch's hired thug. Something disconcertingly magical. Despite her situation, she smiled at the memory of their brief encounter near the canyon.

A conversation she had had with Captain Gitch months before resonated in her mind, '*...As much as I believe Henga has elven roots, I also believe Scruff is descended from giants.*'

For no reason she could put a finger on, she shuddered. All the talk of witches, elves, giants, dwarfs and their run-in with the troll unnerved her. As far as she was concerned, most of the mythical creatures that were rumoured to have existed a long time ago, had been eradicated from the land. If she were to believe some of the villagers, those races were nothing more than creations born from the active imaginations of elders and children.

A deep shiver gripped her and wouldn't let go. The damp fish net wasn't keeping the chill at bay. She sat up properly and gazed longingly at the warehouse, wondering whether her father would come after her tonight or wait on the morrow. Whatever the case, she knew in her heart, she could never go home.

Swallowing her pride, she steadied herself in the dory and climbed onto the dock, hesitantly making her way along the rickety structure.

She took a deep breath and grabbed the handle to the warehouse door; cringing as its hinges disturbed the tranquility of the night. She thought to ask Gitch why he didn't oil them, but gazing over her shoulder at the dark beach, she nodded. They provided security.

The warehouse lay in darkness except for a flickering glow shining through the office window.

Thankful for the relative warmth the warehouse provided, she stared at the office door. Did the captain ever sleep? If she were to knock on the door, he would no doubt wonder why she was there, and that was something she wasn't prepared to talk about. Perhaps she could find an out-of-the-way corner and lie down for the night.

She lifted a boot and froze in midstride.

The office door opened, sconce light flooding the short walkway between it and the exterior door.

Sadyra almost squeaked in fright at the vision of Scruff's silhouette framed in the doorway.

His gaze lingered for but a moment before he disappeared back into the office.

Sadyra stared at the open door. She considered fleeing, but admonished herself. Though she had gotten off to a rough start with the crew, for the most part, they had been good to her. Sure, there were a few who made no bones about their feelings of her presence on the ocean with them, but they hadn't gone out of their way to make her life difficult since the night she had started the brawl in the *Witch's Cauldron.*

Pushing aside her hesitation, she approached the office. It would be good to vent to Gitch.

She was ill-prepared by the sight awaiting her. Scruff lounged in the captain's chair with a blanket draped over his broad shoulders. Of Gitch, there was no sign.

"Oh." She grabbed onto the door jamb. "I'm sorry. I thought Gitch was here."

Scruff regarded her beneath a heavy brow. His intense eyes indicated for her to assume the only other chair in the room.

The urge to run twitched along her limbs, but she resisted its pull. She entered the office; not closing the door, just in case.

She had no sooner sat down than Scruff threw off his blanket, stepped around the desk, and pulled the door shut with a bang.

He resumed his place in the captain's chair and raised his eyebrows as if to ask what she wanted.

Her eyes fell on the closed door. If not for the fact that her father might be lurking somewhere in the village, she would have got up and left, but something in the back of her mind welcomed the close quarters. She forced herself to gaze at the face hidden behind Scruff's unruly beard. "Where's the captain?"

Scruff's eyes narrowed. "Not here."

"I see that."

An uncomfortable silence settled between them until Scruff grunted. "Your father?"

She swallowed and gave a small nod.

"You're safe. For now, at least. He won't dare come in as long as I'm here."

Sadyra pondered his words. She doubted anyone in the village would go against Scruff, but something in his tone hinted at something deeper.

Not knowing what to say, she stared at her hands folded in her lap.

"You're a strange one Sadyra Ors."

She nodded to her hands.

"I feared they were wrong about you, and yet, over the last few months, I've learned to understand why they placed so much importance on you."

Sadyra looked up. She could tell by the way he spoke, *they*, were people other than the crew.

"Aye. I see it now. In your eyes and the way you carry yourself. As much as I know your experience up at the canyon scared you, you handled it quite well considering." He held her gaze and nodded. "You are indeed descended from Pecklyn Ors."

She frowned and looked to the rough ceiling boards is if that would help her discover the relevance of that name. "Pecklyn Ors?"

Scruff's hard glare softened. "You haven't heard of the great Pecklyn?"

She shook her head.

"Explains a lot. I imagine your parents are to blame for that."

The entire conversation seemed bizarre. "Who *are* you?"

"No one of significance."

"That's informative."

His gaze hardened. "What's important here, is you."

"Me?"

"Aye. And the first thing you must learn is that life is tough."

His words flabbergasted her sensibilities. "Do you know what I've gone through my entire life? How my parents…" The brimming tears blurring her vision infuriated her. "*Beat* me?"

He held her gaze.

"I can't remember the last time they weren't drunk and angry. And for what? To harbour some dark secret they refuse to share?" She stood and leaned over the desk, pointing a finger at him. "How dare you tell me I don't know what tough is."

The wide grin on his face choked off her tirade.

"You think that's funny?"

"Not at all. In fact, I find it totally reprehensible."

His matter-of-fact comment stunned her. "Then what are you laughing at?"

"I'm not laughing. I'm happy…" He held up a hand to stay her. "Happy that you've finally come into your own. You've learned a lot in the last few months."

A puzzled expression replaced her frown.

"While working with the crew you have learned the basics of defending yourself." He nodded. "Aye, I've been watching. You're tougher than you think. But, as good as that may be, it's how you deal with adversity that's marked you as someone to be taken seriously."

She sat down, confused. "What are you talking about? I joined the crew to pay back the captain and buy a boat to replace the one I wrecked. I haven't done anything special. Heck, I can't even keep up with Slick when it comes to my duties here."

"You're missing the point. Most of us do the best we can. I can lift more than anyone else. Slim is by far the best fisherman. Slick, the finest navigator and predictor of weather. We all have our strengths."

The rare smile on his face actually made him look pleasant, but she had no idea where his speech was going.

His tone became serious. "We all have weaknesses as well."

She waited for him to elaborate on what her weakness was, but he surprised her.

"You on the other hand, have proven yourself worthy at whatever you set your mind to. No matter the obstacles that stand in your way."

"Pfft. Like what, for instance."

"Like the way you ingratiated yourself with the crew."

She laughed, recalling her first few days.

"You laugh, but I'm serious. When Slick attacked you on the beach, the captain asked who had started the fight. Do remember your response?"

She thought hard. "I think I told him it was my fault."

"Not in those words, but yes, you took responsibility for the fight."

"It was my word against everyone else's. What else could I have done?"

"Nevertheless, you didn't squeal on your mates."

The irony made her smile. "Mates? Ya, right."

Scruff shrugged. "And then, when someone spat on you, and the captain demanded to know who, you could've turned the man in. From what I could tell, he was giving you the most grief, but you didn't."

He raised a single brow and nodded. "That act alone earned you the admiration of many in the crew." He held up a hand to cut off her response. "But, the brawl in the tavern is what won over your most ardent dissenters. You put yourself in harm's way to come to the aid of the very man who had attacked you without provocation that first day on the beach. That act alone proved to them that you were someone they wanted to have in their fold."

Her cheeks reddened. "Well, the fight was my fault."

"You see! That's exactly the attitude that has gained our respect. You shoulder the blame to deflect it from others." He held up his hand again. "Let me finish. Whether consciously or not, you take responsibility for your actions no matter the cost to yourself. That brute in the *Cauldron* should have been taken to task long before you stepped in. I'm as guilty as the next. I stood by and let it happen. The fault is on all of us—as should be the burden of making reparation to the *Cauldron's* owner."

Scruff's words rendered Sadyra speechless. All she could do was watch as he pulled open the thong on a pouch at his belt and produced a handful of copper coins.

He dropped them on the desk before her. "This is by no means enough to make amends for the *Cauldron*, but it is freely given by several members of the crew. I understand they will continue to chip in until your bill is paid in full."

She stared dumbfounded.

"Go ahead. Take it."

Tears slid down her cheeks. She reached out with shaking hands and scooped up the coins. She couldn't recall a time in her life that anyone had ever done anything so kind for her.

It was hard to see through her tears, but if she didn't know better, she would have sworn that Scruff appeared on the verge himself. His breaking voice confirmed her suspicion.

Sadyra

"Never forget this one, very important rule. If you wish to survive, you need to keep proving that you are tougher than life."

Sadyra

To Live Another Day

Hinges squealed from somewhere seemingly far away. Startled awake, Sadyra's eyes were met with complete darkness. It took a moment to comprehend where she was. The sound of excited chatter from beyond the office walls made her sit up between the desk and the chair and listen. "Scruff?"

"I hear it." Scruff's deep voice sounded from the far side of the desk. His chair scraped on the floor and the desk lurched as he struggled to get past it to the door.

He flung it open. "Cap?"

"Something's going down at the *Cauldron*!" Captain Gitch's voice sounded from the warehouse. "Sounds like Tural Ors has gone berserk!"

A cold wave a fear crawled along Sadyra's skin. The colour draining from her face, she tried to see Scruff in the faint light coming from beyond the office door.

"You stay here. Let us deal with him." With that said, he was gone.

Long after the squealing hinges marked Scruff and the captain's departure, Sadyra cowered on the floor, unable to stop her body from trembling. Her father was terrorizing the villagers and it was her fault. She should have known better than to upset him, especially after he had consumed alcohol. If anyone was seriously hurt because of his actions, she would never forgive herself.

Scruff's words mocked her. *'...You shoulder the blame to deflect it from others...it's how you deal with adversity that's marked you as someone to be taken seriously.'*

A bitter laugh escaped her lips. If they could only see her now. Frightened and paralyzed by fear.

Numb, she had no perception of time. At one point she heard raised voices outside, passing between the warehouse and the bay, but she couldn't understand what they said.

A long, eerie squeal jarred her senses. Someone had entered the warehouse. Scruff and the captain would be returning from the *Witch's Cauldron.* She wanted to get up, but dreaded what they would report.

She stared at the office door. It didn't open. The longer she waited, the more concerned she became. Sitting in the dark, her imagination ran roughshod over her.

She shuddered and pushed herself into the corner, trying desperately to vanish into the woodwork. If it was the captain or Scruff, they would have come straight to the office to let her know what had happened.

On hands and knees, she crawled around the desk, cringing as her hip bumped into the shelving along the wall, and peeked above the bottom of the windowsill. The warehouse lay in darkness. Nothing moved.

Allowing herself to breathe again, she straightened up and froze.

A loud noise clattered somewhere on the warehouse floor. It sounded like someone had kicked over a wooden bucket.

She attempted to throw herself to the side and get out of sight but fell over the captain's chair and slammed against the wall—rattling the office structure.

Panic gripped her. She tripped on the chair again as she shoved the desk sideways and scrambled to the door to throw it open. Standing on the threshold, she surveyed the warehouse interior.

Her blood ran cold.

Sadyra

Visible in the faint light filtering through the open exterior door, the unmistakeable form of her father stared back at her, his old sword in hand.

"I thought I'd find you in here, witch," Tural growled and started toward her. "It's time to exorcise the burden of the Ors' legacy and send you to the nether world."

Whatever he was talking about, Sadyra didn't doubt for a moment that he meant to kill her. She wanted to scream, but found it difficult to breathe.

She calculated the distance to the exit. If she ran, she might make it before him.

"There's no sense running. I won't stop hunting you. This was supposed to happen at the Mating Festival but you went and messed that up. Just like you do with everything else."

Sadyra took a step toward the door.

"Bano's parents have committed Bano to offer his unsullied wife as a sacrifice. Thus, we shall appease the dragon gods and lift the family curse from our generation."

Nothing her father said made sense. She shook her head. As much as she didn't want to marry Bano Shell, she had grown to like him for who he was. Though impetuous and incorrigible, he had always been kind to her. If what her father said was true, Bano had been playing her all along.

She swallowed her horror. If the Shell's were aware of the dark secret her parents harboured, that likely meant others were as well. Perhaps the entire village. The implications staggered her. That included the captain and his crew. They had been leading her along all this time to ensure she made it to the Mating Festival.

She took another step; wide eyes never leaving the dark form of her father as he lifted his sword in preparation of a strike.

"Typical Sadyra," Tural snarled. "Always making things difficult. According to legend, we're supposed to wait until your twenty-first name day, but I don't think your mother or

I can take it that long. We'll just have to take our chances with Sable."

The starry sky was visible beyond the doorway. Her father's words hypnotized her as she tried to understand their meaning. Nothing he said made sense. She had heard the elders' tales of the dark rituals that had been performed on the Summoning Stone in the past, but couldn't recall hearing of one in her lifetime. The mention of Sable chilled her to the bone. She took another step.

Tural matched her movement. "Twice you almost ruined everything. If you had died on the reef the day you wrecked the boat, you would've burdened us with another twelve years of drudgery. But, dealing with you now, I curse the sea gods the kraken spared you."

The boat! She needed to get to it. She had to distract him long enough to get free of the warehouse.

"You lie. Bano would never harm me. He loves me."

An evil laugh rumbled deep within Tural's throat. "Don't kid yourself. He already possesses the sacred dagger. The only thing that boy cares about is himself." Tural nodded. "And, his insatiable desire to learn about our family heritage."

She gaped as she recalled the fancy hilted blade hanging from Bano's belt.

The feel of her knife in her hand surprised her. She took another sideways step and held it out. "Don't come any closer."

"What're going to do with that? Clean your nails?"

Her feet were moving almost before she knew it.

"Hey!" Tural charged.

She slipped through the door; banging off the jamb. The sound of Tural's sword biting into the doorframe made her stagger across the walkway that ran the length of the building. Not daring to look back, she ran toward the dock.

Tural burst through the door; pausing long enough to spot her, and gave chase.

Her boat was tied off. She would never cast off fast enough before he was on her. Sprinting past the jetty, she made her way to the far corner of the warehouse and ran onto the commons; her mind spinning with questions of where to go.

The *Witch's Cauldron* loomed to the south, just beyond the temple. Thinking about her father's revelation that the villagers were aware of his intentions, she doubted she had any *real* friends anywhere.

It was difficult to believe that the captain and Scruff were in on it, but she couldn't afford to be wrong. She had been mistaken about Bano, and she had known him her whole life.

Boots crunching gravel, she contemplated running down the mountain trail toward Thunderhead. The sight of several men exiting the *Witch's Cauldron* in a hurry and running toward her, changed her mind.

Scruff pointed. "There she is!"

The giant man, accompanied by Gitch and several others, ran at her.

Her mind spun. How this could be happening?

Left with no choice, she ran as fast as her panic would carry her toward the two buildings on the far side of the mercantile, hoping to reach the north trail.

Tural raced around the corner.

"Stop!" Voices rang off the cliff face behind the village.

Sadyra passed the north corner of the warehouse and slid to a stop. Slim and Slick emerged from the shadows between the buildings she ran toward.

Slick's nasally voice reached her. "There she is!"

Much faster than Tural, she had created a good distance between them. She searched the beach for somewhere to hide. The dark hulks of Captain Gitch's fleet were pulled high on the shore, but that would only serve to trap her. Hazarding a quick glance at her father, halfway along the warehouse and closing fast, she bolted around the fishery, sprinting down its walkway. Left with no other choice, she hammered up the jetty and jumped into her boat—her momentum nearly pitching her over the side.

It took a couple of anxious moments to saw through the ropes securing the bow and stern, but as her keen edge severed the second rope, she shoved off and dropped the oar blades into the water. Rowing hard, she put distance between the small dory and the jetty and veered toward where she could only guess the gap in the reef lie shrouded in darkness.

Clouds swirled across the moon, making it hard to discern the crags protruding from the rolling waves. She slowed her approach. It wouldn't do to wreck another boat.

Footsteps pounded along the jetty.

"Sadyra, stop! We got him."

The sound of Captain Gitch's voice brought tears to her eyes. How could she have let herself be sucked into his part of the grand scheme of maintaining the dark secret? Angry with herself for being so stupid, she rowed harder.

"Go after her!" The captain's words carried across the water, confirming her suspicion.

Steering her craft toward the gap in the reef, she watched several men run down the jetty and along the shore. It would take them time to overturn their large boats and drag them across the stony beach. The mucky ocean floor exposed by the low tide would make their task that much more difficult.

A swell lifted her boat and carried it toward the reef. She compensated with frantic oar strokes and aimed her bow at where she believed the middle of the gap lie.

Slick's estimation of an incoming weather front was proving accurate as usual. The surf had picked up considerably since she had hidden in her boat earlier in the night.

"Sadie! Stop!"

She glared at the captain waving his arms from the end of the pier. How dare he call her by her nickname? She hoped a rogue wave would wash him into the ocean.

Her attention divided between the captain and those struggling on the beach to manhandle their boats into the water, she almost rowed past the gap. Her dory slipped down the backside of a large wave that had broken on the reef right beside her.

The next wave broke over the bow, lifting her boat and spinning it out of control. She plied her oars with everything she had, expertly bringing the bow to bear on the open water beyond the gap.

She believed she had navigated the dangerous stretch but as her boat slid down the backside of the ensuing wave, a sudden jarring nearly cost Sadyra her grip on one of the oars. Caught in an eddy around the jagged rock, the sound she dreaded could be clearly heard over the roar of the crashing waves. Timbers cracked as the boat lurched sideways.

She screeched, fully expecting the dory to fall apart but the pull of the next wave dragged the boat free. Rowing hard, she had one chance to escape the yawning teeth of the reef. If the rapidly building wave that formed in the wake of the last one broke before it reached her, she would be thrown into the unforgiving jags.

Push. Pull. Push. Pull. As fast as she could, she rowed for her life.

The dory lifted out of the trough and rose toward the wave's crest. Just a few more strokes and she would be clear.

White froth burst into life along the wave's ridge; approaching her in a violent rush. Helpless, she held her breath and prayed to the sea gods that the kraken wouldn't take her tonight.

Her boat teetered on the top of the wave; her oar blades unable to touch the water as it broke beneath the keel.

A violent crash of spray and turbulent water erupted before her eyes. Her boat slipped down the backside of the wave—the wood-rending reef disappearing beneath the swell.

Her oars lifted in her hands as they touched water again. Not sparing a moment to check on the progress of the chase boats, Sadyra put her back into propelling her craft out to sea.

She didn't know how long she rowed, fighting the northerly current and rising seas, but by the time she rested long enough to take an accounting of her surroundings, she couldn't see anything besides the endless sea and the dark shoreline south of Fishmonger Bay. If Captain Gitch's crew had been able to follow her beyond the reef, the darkening skies prevented her from seeing them.

The abrasions she had picked up during her frenzied flight down the steep hill earlier in the night stung in the salt water that soaked her to the skin.

Water filled the bottom of her boat at an alarming rate. The keel had been cracked on the reef, but there was nothing to be done about it. Reefs littered the coastline. She would have to ply on and hope to reach Thunderhead before her boat succumbed to the water it took in.

She stretched out her aching shoulders and back; taking a moment to flex her fingers several times. Regripping the oar handles, she began the arduous task of propelling her boat toward Thunderhead; thankful she had been given the chance to live another day.

As the dory lifted and lowered over the endless waves in the darkness, she was at the mercy of her thoughts. She fought to see through blinding tears. Of all of her hurts, Scruff's betrayal hit her the hardest. She had naively entertained fantasies involving her and the gruff sailor—envisioning a life together. She gritted her teeth at her foolishness and threw her back into the oars.

Sadyra

To Catch a Tiger

Sunrise greeted Sadyra's broken boat floundering in the northerly current of the Niad Ocean. She intended on putting in at the North Shore Fishery with the hope of finding a friendly face, but by the time the dawn's early light sufficiently illuminated the coastline, she realized she had almost floated right by Thunderhead. As the shoreline clarified, she found herself looking at the wide inlet to Thunderhead Fjord.

Summoning her last bit of strength, she turned the boat around and made for the calmer waters beyond the natural break wall that protruded from the northern tip of the fjord's mouth—the line of jumbled rock jutting out from beneath the wall of a multiple-storied building.

Her boat had taken on so much water, she was amazed it floated at all. Although desperately seeking the comfort of a familiar face in the aftermath of the troubling events in Fishmonger Bay, she didn't dare risk remaining on the turbulent ocean longer than necessary. Thankfully, the stormfront that had threatened overnight had passed north of Thunderhead, but the heavy seas left in its wake made it difficult to keep her little boat on course.

She craned her neck to ensure she aimed the bow properly and marvelled at the sheer size of the port city of Thunderhead. In all her years of sailing, she had never ventured as far as the fjord by sea. The view from her current vantage point of the sprawling city that dominated the north shore left her breathless. Layer upon layer of jumbled buildings climbed the foothills fronting the massive bulk of a mountain that easily dwarfed Peril's Peak back home.

Entering the mouth of the fjord, dozens of piers jutted into the calmer stretch of water; its gentle current noticeable in her weary state. Each oar stroke felt like it would be her last, but somehow she found the strength to lift the oars again.

Grey stone buildings mixed with wooden warehouses lined the high bank of the shoreline at the end of each boat infested dock. Men and women crawled over the boats and docks alike—an army of ants, unloading and stowing wares. Fisheries and buildings belonging to the well-to-do dominated the waterfront, their facades partially hidden behind the bulk of tall ships sporting lofty masts and spider webbed with dizzying mazes of rope.

She fretted that the piers were too big for her to put in. The rugged shoreline at the base of the pilings, partially visible beyond the large boats, didn't instill her with hope. If her boat wrecked on the rocks, she honestly believed she didn't have the strength to swim in her clothing and boots. Nor was she willing to part with them. They were all she had to her name. With the exception of the coppers Scruff had handed to her, any money she had earned while in Gitch's employ had been divvied between paying for the captain's net, reimbursing the owner of the *Witch's Cauldron*, and satisfying her parents.

An official looking pier passed by on her right—two ominous warships moored by themselves against a wide dock. Several men clad in armour and livery matching the green and red pennants flapping atop towering masts, patrolled the jetty—curious eyes watching the progress of her floundering boat up the fjord.

Sadyra

As the northern banks of the inland waterway rose up to match those of the uninhabitable southern shore, the large piers gave way to curving jetties low to the water.

Sadyra chose the last one; gratefully accepting the assistance of an old fisherman who knelt and steadied her boat so she could drag herself onto the dock and lay in the early morning light.

Sadyra woke from a restless nap. Glorious sunshine beat down on her where she lay on a flat rock hidden between several large boulders. The old fisherman had allowed her to make use of the spot he had claimed for himself. The grey-bearded man had fed her a meagre fare of fish brine—the taste and smell enough to turn up her nose and make her gag, but she struggled past it—the ocean voyage had taken a lot out of her.

The fisherman had left her alone and went to do whatever he did during the day. She folded his tattered blanket and dug into a hidden pocket inside the lining of her tunic; withdrawing the coins. She placed them in the old, battered pot he used for cooking. It was the least she could do to repay his kindness.

Climbing up a steep embankment, she skirted a couple of rundown buildings and started along a dirt track that soon gave way to a cobblestone roadway, and made her way toward the business district of Thunderhead. She had visited the marketplace many times in the past—with her father at first, but over the past couple of years on her own in an attempt to sell her catch—hoping to garner better coin than Skipper was willing to pay.

Sadyra

She had never been on this side of the marketplace before, but she knew that as long as she kept on the road paralleling the fjord, she would walk straight into it.

Rickety structures gave way to sturdier, taller buildings. The dress of the people walking around transformed from breeks and ratty tunics to men and women in pantaloons and frilly tops. The familiar noise of hawkers peddling their wares drifted up the roadway, easing the apprehension from her dreary mind. Drab tents, colourful awnings, and countless stands helped to take her mind off her troubles.

A trip to see the Skipper and Swab would do her heart good. The old fishery owner had never made a habit of being pleasant—he made no qualms about how he conducted business with women, and yet, aside from underpaying, he had always been decent to her. And then there was his lone worker, Swab. The teenaged boy always greeted her with a smiling face and that was something she dearly needed at the moment.

So caught up in the sights, sounds, and smells of the busy marketplace, complete with pushy merchants calling out to anyone who had the misfortune of coming anywhere near them, she failed to see a group of four shirtless men clad in matching brown leather breeks, standing around a table laden with buckets and fish. Four men who, if she looked closer, she would have realized before it was too late that she had seen them recently. The tallest and skinniest of the group pointed and said something to his companions before darting away.

She followed the man with her eyes until the crowd swallowed him up. Thinking hard, it dawned on her that he was the man who had stood behind the brute in the *Witch's Cauldron* that night she had instigated the great fight. She turned in time to witness the approach of the other three men. Sailors belonging to the brute's crew.

"Well, well, well. Look who we have here. The wench from Fishmonger Bay who couldn't keep her nose out of Ivar's business."

The name, Ivar, rang a bell. Her father had mentioned it at the table a couple of months ago when Captain Gitch had walked her home. At the time, she thought Gitch had been doing her a favour by keeping her company in her father's presence. Looking back, the treacherous man had been playing his part in Tural's grand scheme to eradicate his dark secret.

She tried to walk around the men, but two of them darted forward and grabbed her by the wrists.

The last man snorted, "Not so fast, missy. I'm thinking the Blade will want a few words with you."

Those people closest to them in the crowded market stepped back, allowing the men room to drag her toward their stall.

"What are you talking about?" She pulled against their hold, but couldn't free herself from their iron grip. She dug in her heels. "Let me go!"

The men yanked on her arms, almost lifting her from her feet.

The burly man snickered. "The Blade likes spirited lasses."

It took a moment to understand what the burly man implied. With a desperate shove, she drove the stocky man into the table displaying their goods.

Unable to stop himself, the burly sailor released her arm in a desperate attempt to prevent himself from falling over the table. A table leg broke under his weight, sending the table, man, and buckets of fish to the ground with a mighty crash.

Sadyra grabbed onto the other man's wrist and pried at his fingers, but she couldn't wrest her arm free.

The third man latched onto her, trapping her free arm.

The usual noises of the crowded marketplace were replaced by an expectant hush. A large circle of spectators had formed around Sadyra and her three attackers.

The burly man jumped to his feet, wiping away the debris covering him; a broken table leg in hand. He circled around and stood in the middle of the gathering crowd.

His companions dragged Sadyra away from the overturned table, doing their best to hang onto her as she pulled and yanked; twisting and kicking.

Bystanders voiced encouragement for the battle to heat up. Ill mannered people shouted vulgar slurs at both Sadyra and the men struggling to hang on.

The bare-chested man brandishing the table leg slapped the wooden spindle against the palm of his free hand, and searched for an opening.

Sadyra bounced back and forth on the balls of her feet, preparing to dodge as best she could while being restrained. One or two shots from the table leg would be enough to seriously injure her. As he closed in, she spat and kicked out, driving him back.

"Hold her steady, damn you!" The man growled at his companions.

Sadyra pulled hard, bringing one of her captor's arms close enough to bite.

He screamed his displeasure and released her.

Spinning on the other, she ignored his painful grip and kicked him between the legs. Before he knew what was happening, she followed up with her other boot.

The man released her, bending over to grab at his injury.

Sadyra

Sadyra's boot connected with his face, lifting him backward. He hit the ground hard and didn't move.

The man she had bitten, shouted and charged. As he closed on her, realization of what she held in her hand, twisted his face in terror. He ducked to the side but wasn't fast enough to avoid Sadyra's knife.

In one fluid motion, Sadyra stepped into her lunge and slid the blade under the man's ribs. He dropped to cobblestones, writhing in agony.

Not missing a beat, Sadyra located the last man, who gaped at her, still brandishing the table leg.

The man's shocked gaze flicked from one of his injured companions to the other. Holding his hands in the air, he let the table leg clatter to the ground.

Sadyra scanned the crowd, turning one way and then another, searching for any more of the crew. Her frantic gaze paused on the largest man she had ever seen.

Dressed in a brass cuirass, a neatly-trimmed, red-bearded giant watched on—a great smile splitting his chiselled features. His throaty laugh sounded above the stunned silence that had settled over the crowd, "Hah, hah, hah!"

Pointing at Sadyra, the giant glanced at a tall, slender brunette and proclaimed, "She's the one. You two are going to make a mighty fine fighting pair."

Larina and Lozen burst from the far end of the alley, nearly running headlong into Pollard's broad backside. The giant, resplendent in his brass cuirass, stood with his arms crossed and his head nodding.

Larina was taller than most, but she had to stand on her toes to see what was so enthralling. A large crowd had gathered, the people shouting encouragement and jibes at four combatants squaring off in the middle of what appeared to be a marketplace judging by the tables and tents displaying all sorts of wares.

Forcing her way to the front of the crowd, she watched as two men clad only in tan, leather breeks, held an auburn-haired woman by the arms.

A bare-chested, husky man, wearing the same coloured breeks as the others, held what appeared to be a table leg in his hands and taunted the young woman with it.

Bouncing on the balls of a pair of knee-high boots, the woman's storm-grey eyes glared hatred at the man; gnashing her teeth and spitting—kicking out whenever he got near.

Larina glanced up at Pollard's enrapt stare. "We've got to help her. They'll rip her apart."

Pollard never took his intense gaze from the fight, but his tone was firm. "Nay, lass. This is not our fight. I have a feeling those poor men are about to find out what happens to people who try to catch a tiger."

Larina frowned, but heeded his words.

The young woman's skin glistened with sweat as she fought to free herself from her captor's grasp.

The man with the table leg moved in to take a swing, but dodged back again, barely missing eating the toe of her boot.

"Hold her steady, damn you!" The man growled at his companions who were struggling to maintain their grip.

The man with the table leg had no sooner spoken than the growling woman bit one man's arm and pulled free of his grasp. Spinning on the other, she kicked him between the legs, not once, but twice.

The second man released her and doubled over in agony only to receive a third kick to the face that straightened him out as he flew backward; landing in a heap.

The man nursing a bleeding arm where the woman's teeth had punctured his skin, ran at her, cursing. His eyes opened wide—trying get out of harm's way as he spotted the knife in her hand.

The woman stepped into her lunge and drove the knife up and underneath his ribs.

An agonized gasp escaped his lips. He fell to the ground clutching his stomach, writhing in pain.

The woman wasted no time turning wild eyes on the man holding the table leg.

The man looked from one of his companions to another, his mouth opened wide in shock. He held up his hands in surrender, the table leg slipping through his fingers and clattering on the cobblestones.

The woman searched the crowd, adjusting her bladed stance one way and then another, as if daring anyone else to come at her.

"Hah, hah, hah!"

Pollard's throaty laugh made Larina look up at the wide grin splitting his face. He pointed to the woman glaring death at the crowd. "She's the one!"

He placed a huge mitt on Larina's shoulder. "You two are going to make a mighty fine fighting pair."

Larina frowned at him, thinking, *'Not bloody likely.'*

Sadyra

Kindred Spirits

Larina walked behind Pollard and Lozen as they approached the woman brandishing a bloody knife. The auburn-haired young woman had already proven she wasn't afraid to use it. If Larina had to guess the woman's age, she would hazard the girl behind those storm-grey eyes was in her late teens.

If Pollard thought she was going to become fast friends with the crazed woman, he had best think again. The Storms End Lightning Bolt worked alone. It was easier that way. Responsible only for herself, Larina didn't have to worry about someone else's back. Being a thief and lockpick, she had learned the art of being deathly quiet and quick. Having to worry about someone else while performing a potentially deadly task would slow her down and inevitably lead to mistakes.

"Easy, lass." Pollard held his hands out in front of him, trying to show the woman he wasn't a threat.

Larina shook her head. She sighed and grabbed his elbow with both hands, pulling him to a halt. "Easy yourself, big fella." She stepped in front of him, eyeing him from head to foot; shaking her head. "You're big enough to scare a troll from a corpse. Look at you. Eighteen feet and busting with muscle."

She flashed the crazed teen a fake smile. "Not the brightest, these giant types."

The teen glanced from Larina to Pollard to Lozen and back again. "Don't come any closer." Her eyes flicked to the man she had stabbed as she backed toward the upturned table. “If you’re part of Ivar the Blade’s crew, I’ll gut you.”

Larina backed off a step. Pulling her dagger free, she pointed it at the woman. “I don’t take kindly to people threatening me.” She held out a hand to keep Pollard from advancing. “I don’t know who this Igor is but—”

“Ivar.”

“Whoever. We don’t know him. We’ve just got in from Storms End and…” She shrugged and stepped aside. “I’ll let Pollard tell you.”

As Larina moved aside, she winked at the woman and whispered, “Don’t worry. The big oaf is a pussy cat.” She waggled her dagger. “But remember. *I’m* watching you.”

Pollard stepped forward and started to say something but paused and gave Larina an odd look. He turned his light blue eyes back to the teen, considering the knife she held. “I am Pollard Banebridge; son of Thoril Half-Hand, the Master of the Storms End Council.”

The teen glanced between Larina and Pollard, obviously having no idea who Pollard or his father were. Her frightened eyes fell on Lozen.

Lozen’s smiling face radiated warmth. “You don’t need to fear us. We’re here to find a warrior. You’re a warrior, no?”

The teen frowned, lowering her knife. “You have me mistaken with someone else.”

“No.” Pollard shook his head. “I’m pretty sure you’re the one I’ve been looking for.”

Larina’s expression matched the teen’s, both of them pausing to stare at the giant. He had told Larina *she* was the one he’d been looking for. Just because this teenager fought like a cornered badger didn’t mean she was worthy enough to be included in their company. Anyone with half a mind would react like the teen had if they were threatened by the likes of those bare-chested men.

“You don’t even know me. I’m not from around here.” The teen searched the crowd as if looking for someone. “If you don't mind, I'd like to be away from here before more of these people show up." She pointed her knife at the burly man who was easing himself into the crowd.

Pollard followed her gaze. "You needn't worry about him. *Or* anyone else he may be associated with. If you agree to listen to what I have to say, I'll make sure you never have to worry about them again."

Larina sheathed her dagger. Clearly, the young woman was frightened.

The teen looked Pollard over, her gaze resting on the sword hilt protruding over his shoulder. She cast a final look around the crowd, and nodded.

Lozen held out a hand.

The teen backed away a step, on the verge of bolting into the crowd behind her. "Where are we going?"

"To the ship to talk." Lozen wiggled her fingers for the teen to grab onto.

The teen hesitantly accepted Lozen's hand, and followed the warrior across the marketplace toward two officious looking buildings. They stopped at the entrance to a broad laneway warded by eight guards. Upon seeing Pollard, the guardsmen retracted their polearms, permitting them access to the military docks.

Larina fell in behind the newcomer, going over her with a critical eye. Slim, attractive, not afraid to assert herself in the face of danger, the teen appeared hardened beyond her years.

Larina reluctantly admitted that perhaps the young woman might indeed be someone to be taken seriously. But, if Pollard entertained the idea that they were to become partners in whatever he had in mind for them at Songsbirth, the big oaf was in for a rude awakening.

Sadyra

Scruff's daunting presence cut through the crowd gathered about the Thunderhead marketplace. He had walked from the North Shore Fishery, searching for Sadyra Ors. The sight of the young woman pointing her bloodied knife at a giant man and his two female companions stopped him in his tracks.

He felt for the dagger he kept hidden beneath his tunic as he observed an exotic-looking woman dressed in tan suede—a headband bearing a single feather keeping her lengthy black hair from her face—reach out a hand.

He could tell by Sadyra's reaction how leery the gesture made her, but in the end, Sadyra accepted the woman's hand and allowed herself to be led across the marketplace toward the docks.

Scruff followed several paces behind, but they passed beyond a point patrolled by the city Watch. His heart heavy, he stopped and nodded. Sadyra Ors was one hell of a woman, but any thoughts of the two of them sharing a future had been nothing more than a foolish fantasy. It was time to return to South March to report to the elven council.

He would have to accept the fact that any notion he might have had of developing a deeper relationship with the runt, wasn't meant to be.

Standing amongst a small group of people, most of whom she had never seen before, Sadyra studied the fine workmanship of the *Crusher*. Though smaller than the three warships docked around her, the *Crusher* had the appearance of a sleek, more refined ocean-going vessel.

She searched every new face that came on deck, expecting to see Ivar the Blade or one of his crew, but so far, no one fit their description.

The giant, Pollard, issued orders, and the men and women surrounding them went their separate ways.

Pollard seemed friendly enough despite his daunting size. She pitied anyone going up against him; even Scruff. She smiled to herself. She would love to see Scruff and Pollard tangle. It would serve the Fishmonger Bay man right, after the way he had manoeuvred her into thinking he wasn't such a bad guy. Of all of the people who had betrayed her, she didn't think she would ever get over Scruff's deception. Though she was loath to admit it, she had developed strong feelings for the gruff man—ones that she had never experienced with anyone else. Reflecting on those heartbreaking emotions, she felt stupid.

Her gaze settled on Lozen. Apparently, Lozen was a warrior from a group of people known as Indians—whatever that meant. Apart from Lozen's darker skin and glistening hair that was blacker than midnight, the woman didn't appear different than anyone else.

Of the three people who had approached her in the marketplace, the tall brunette with freckles around large brown eyes, and clad entirely in black, struck her as the most intriguing. Pollard had introduced her as Larina, but had said no more. Not where she was from, and no last name. She was just, Larina.

For some reason, Larina gave Sadyra the feeling that she didn't care for her presence aboard the *Crusher*. The lanky woman couldn't be much older than herself, but the way she flicked her long bangs from her face gave Sadyra the impression that Larina was full of herself. She begrudgingly conceded that if she were half as pretty as Larina, she would be full of herself as well.

"So, young lady. Before we go any further, what do we call you?"

The deep, male voice pulled her attention to the beaming face of the giant. Embarrassed, she realized she had been staring at Larina. Searching the remaining faces around her, she blushed and stammered, "You…you can call me Sadyra."

"Just Sadyra?" Pollard asked.

"Um…yes. *Just* Sadyra." She wanted nothing to do with her last name.

"See?" Pollard playfully punched Larina in the shoulder. "You two are more alike than you know."

The punch knocked Larina sideways. She grabbed her shoulder, scowling.

"Ha! Take more than a closed fist to hurt the Lightning Bolt." His expression turned serious as he turned his attention back on Sadyra. "Care to tell us what happened in the marketplace?"

Sadyra couldn't make sense of the talk of lightning bolts. She shook her head. "No. Not really."

"Do your parents know where you are?"

Sadyra snorted. "Who cares?"

Lozen stepped close. "Is Sadyra in trouble?"

The way the warrior's eyes bore into her, Sadyra felt as if her soul had been laid bare. A shudder coursed through her. "You could say that."

"You want Lozen to find Sadyra's parents?"

The warrior's accent was hard to understand. "If you mean, do I want you to get my parents for me, the answer is no."

Lozen nodded as if she understood. She bowed her head to Sadyra and spoke to Pollard. "She needs you."

Sadyra frowned. "Look. I don't know who you people are. I appreciate that you mean well, but I really must be going." She looked to the gangplank.

Pollard's voice stopped her from moving. "You're running from something. Something isn't right between you and your parents."

"That's an understatement. But yes, you could say that."

"Can I be of assistance to smooth things over?"

Sadyra stared at the deck planks between them and muttered, "Not unless you know how to exorcise a dragon witch."

"What's that?"

"Nothing." Sadyra lifted sad eyes to meet Pollard's. "I should leave. I don't want to cause trouble."

Lozen grabbed Sadyra's hands. "Sadyra is no trouble. Lozen will watch over you."

Sadyra swallowed. Not much of what Lozen said made sense, but she appreciated the sincerity in her voice.

"If I remain here, trouble will find me. If not from the friends of the man I stabbed, then I suspect from the city Watch."

"Pfft." Larina scoffed. "I'll deal with the Watch."

Sadyra considered Larina's words. Her bravado was fine and well, but she doubted Larina wished to tangle with the city guard.

Pollard pulled his sword from over his shoulders—two separate sword blades fused into one guard.

Sadyra gaped at the magnificent weapon. Seeing Pollard's muscles bulging, she doubted she could lift the sword.

"No one will bother you in my presence, aboard *my* ship. As third in command of the Songsbirthian Guard, and son of Thoril Half-Hand, you can rest assured, you are safe aboard the *Crusher*."

Sadyra tried to convince herself that she could trust the sincerity in Pollard's tone, but a faint voice in the back of her mind warned her to be wary of a silver-tongued stranger. She had been duped too many times to take him at face value. And yet, she couldn't escape her gut feeling that there was something different about the giant and the warrior woman, and it was okay to lower her guard.

Bano, Gitch, and Scruff had filled her with the same warm feelings—leaving her devastated at how badly that had turned out. The fact that Gitch had claimed Scruff was descended from giants did little to bolster her trust in Pollard's company.

She felt so alone. She didn't know who to trust. She wasn't sure she trusted herself to make the right decision.

Her run in with Ivar's crew had unsettled her greatly. If nothing else, it taught her that Thunderhead wasn't far enough removed from Fishmonger Bay to keep her safe. In order to avoid further trouble, she must travel farther away. With no money and no idea where to go, she felt trapped.

Her concept of the geography of the region wasn't ideal. From the little she knew of the immense kingdom of Zephyr, there was no easy way over The Spine—the vast mountain range spanned the entire west coast of Zephyr. Sailing was the logical choice when traversing the coastal region. Wandering through the mountains without a guide would likely prove a fatal mistake.

She sighed. "Where did you say you were going?"

"Songsbirth," Pollard said.

"And that's a long way from here?"

"A good tenday if conditions are favourable."

"Ten days?" Sadyra thought out loud. "Are there other places along the way?"

"Aye. There's Madrigail Bay. The Forke. Millsford."

"And what would it cost me to travel with you to one of these places?"

"Cost?" Pollard frowned. "Why, nothing. You will be my guest."

"But what if I don't wish to go all the way to Songsbirth?"

Pollard seemed flummoxed.

Lozen squeezed her hands. "It's okay. You go where you go. We'll not stop you." She looked over her shoulder at Pollard. "Right, master?"

Pollard appeared like he wanted to protest. "Well, um, I guess. But—"

Lozen interrupted. "There. You see? Pollard is a man of honour."

Sadyra

"You should go talk to her before we reach Madrigail Bay," Pollard said above the noise of the wind and the crash of the waves breaking across the bow. Staring forward from the high quarterdeck, he experienced a feeling he seldom had before. He wasn't sure what it was other than a sadness weighing on his heart for the troubled young woman he had found fighting for her life in the Thunderhead market.

Larina leaned against the port rail, ostensibly watching the rugged coastline pass by on the eastern horizon. If not for the height of The Spine, the land on the horizon would have been lost from sight. She frowned. "Why me? If she's *your* chosen one, you don't need someone like me kicking around."

Pollard's brow knit together. Ever since they had brought Sadyra onboard, Larina hadn't been herself. Though never one to be accused of a bubbly personality, Larina had, up until recently, seemed happy to be included in the group of recruits heading to Songsbirth.

On their travels from the southern ports of Apexceal and Ember Breath, to a short stay in Madrigail Bay, Pollard and his small band of Songsbirthian guardsmen had enlisted dozens of candidates to be considered for placement in the Songsbirthian Guard. More specifically, to bolster the ranks of the Splendoor Catacombs Guard.

Under Master Pul's direction, Pollard had been assigned the task of finding people worthy of the appointment. Not everyone who had been brought aboard the *Crusher* would successfully pass the high standards required to become a member of the Songsbirthian Guard. As strong and ambitious as the selected people were, Pollard doubted half would make the cut.

He prided himself in his ability to judge a person's character and fortitude. Of the recruits who were making the long journey inland, Pollard saw the potential in each one, but past experience had shown him otherwise.

He was certain the feisty brunette at his side would pass the rigourous training regimen and final test without a problem, providing he was able to keep her mind focused on the ordeal ahead.

He was also sure that the young woman standing alone on the bow had the mettle required to become a standout Catacombs Guard. All he had to do was find a way to convince her that she needed them as badly as they needed her. According to his father, and Master Pul, a great storm was brewing in the not too distant future.

He put a hand on Larina's shoulder. "Because, like I said to you before, you two are much alike. I see it in the way you conduct yourselves."

"Please." Larina shrugged out from under his touch and glared. "I'm nothing like her. She's a fisherwoman. I'm a…a…"

"Thief?"

"Sure. Fine. If that's what you think of me."

"I didn't mean it to sound that way."

"Whatever. It doesn't matter. What matters is that I can look after myself, *by* myself. I don't need a partner, nor do I want one."

"If you wish to become part of the guard, you must learn to function as a team."

"I thought you said on the trip down the fjord that my skills are best suited for an advance scout." Her features hardened. "*Scout*." She emphasized the 't'. "One person, not two."

"You're right. I can see you working apart from the main garrison, *but*, I would never send anyone out on their own. You'll be responsible for someone at all times, just as they'll be responsible for you."

"Would've been nice of you to explain that before we hit the ocean."

"Would it have made any difference?"

She shrugged. “Perhaps.”

Pollard shook his head and leaned on the railing; focusing on a high, snow-capped peak directly across from the *Crusher*. The strong spirited men required to do the job of a Songsbirthian Guardsman were generally pig-headed and unruly, but they possessed a certain mental strength that a normal man lacked. When it came to recruiting women, however, Pollard didn’t know if he had the courage to tame the ones that would prove out the best in the long run.

Larina leaned on the rail beside him, her long hair tickling his bare arms in the wind.

He stared at her profile—soft features belying the tiger lurking within. “Ya, well, there’s no guarantee you’ll pass the rigourous test ahead, so perhaps we’re having this discussion for nothing.”

She stared him in the eye but remained quiet.

“*If* you pass the testing—and that’s a big if—you’ll have to work with at least one other, whether you like it or not.”

She ran her tongue behind her upper lip and looked away, clearly unimpressed.

“If I were you, I’d want to be the one who chooses the person watching my back. Your life will depend on it.”

“So. You’re a fisherwoman?” The question sounded as bad as it felt for Larina to speak it as she tried to break the ice with the young woman from Fishmonger Bay.

The sun had set hours ago, leaving the deck of the *Crusher* in the shadows of flickering lantern light, but Sadyra hadn’t moved—one elbow resting on the port rail and the other on the starboard rail as they came together above a bowsprit depicting a rearing kraken.

Sadyra blinked. “Not anymore.”

Larina nodded, trying hard to think of something else to say. “No, huh? Hmm.”

It was all she could do not to walk away. “I’ve never been on the ocean before.”

Sadyra said nothing.

“Ya. Sounds strange, I guess. Especially to someone like you.”

Sadyra shrugged, her gaze on the waves.

Larina gritted her teeth. She recalled the conversation Sadyra had with Pollard. Taking a deep breath, she asked, “Trouble with your parents, eh? That sucks.”

Sadyra tensed.

“Mine wanted nothing to do with me.”

Sadyra’s hard expression softened.

“Ain’t got no idea who my pop is. Don’t think my mother knew either.”

Sadyra turned an inquisitive gaze on her.

“Said he was someone of importance who would someday come for me.” She sighed, mad at herself for exposing her past and allowing her eyes to well with tears. She swallowed and leaned on the starboard rail. “Guess I wasn’t worth the trouble.”

The waves slapped the keel in rhythmic cadence, spraying them from time to time, but never enough to make standing in the cooler night air uncomfortable.

The *Crusher* cut through the heavy seas; taut rigging creaking and sails snapping. A shout from somewhere down the deck was answered by another.

Larina swallowed as Sadyra’s soft voice reached her ears above the noise of the ocean.

“Mine beat me.”

A tingle ran up Larina’s spine. The deep sadness in Sadyra’s tone, palpable.

Larina studied the young woman’s profile; moved by the tears flowing down Sadyra’s freckled cheeks. She put her arm over Sadyra's shoulder and together, they watched the waves break over the bow.

The End

Of part two of the Banebridge Companion novels.
The story concludes in part three: Pollard

Thank you for reading *Sadyra*. I'd be grateful if you would take a moment to leave a review.

If you liked this book, you may also enjoy:

LEGENDS OF THE LURKER SERIES

Reecah's Flight, Book 1
Reecah's Gift, Book 2
Reecah's Legacy, Book 3
Save and buy the Box-set

SOUL FORGE SAGA

Soul Forge, Book 1
Wizard of the North, Book 2
Into the Madness, Book 3
Save and buy the Box-set

Pollard

Enjoy chapter one of *Pollard*: the final book in the Banebridge Companion Novels

A Distant Storm

"A distant storm is brewing on the horizon." Thoril Half-Hand's words resonated in Pollard's head as he watched the waves; a prophetic warning not to be taken lightly. If the son of Thoril the Kraidic Crusher foresaw disaster in the not too distant future, his son, Pollard, would do everything in his power to see to it that those he loved and protected were safe.

Being part giant, whenever Pollard set his mind to something, it was done quickly and efficiently. Fortifying the garrison of Songsbirth against the imminent threat required new recruits, but not just anyone would do. They had to be cut from a different cloth—endowed with the spirit of the ancient warriors who had fought and died for Zephyr in centuries past. Back to the Age of Saints and beyond.

The people Pollard searched for were more often than not outcasts from society. In his years of experience, peculiar quirks and eccentric mannerisms differentiated those who professed the desire to do the right thing and those who were bereft of the common sense that prevented them from placing themselves in the life or death situations his garrison required if the ideals of Zephyr's regime were to survive the imminent cataclysm his father predicted.

Pollard

The southern ports of Apexceal and Ember Breath had netted Pollard's expedition fifteen promising trainees. Of those, he projected that less than half would prove worthy enough to become a Songsbirthian Guard. Of this fact he made no bones about hiding from the recruits. He allayed their apprehension by assuring them that any who failed to make the cut would be sent to join the Royal Guard in the king's city of Carillon.

Pollard's family's flagship, the *Crusher,* sailed clear of the Undying Wall's western isthmus jutting leagues into the heavy seas of the Niad Ocean. Three tall masts bulging with sailcloth carried the sleek, black warship over the water's rough surface—its bow plunging into deep troughs and cutting the backside of the next wave.

A cold spray washed down the main deck; its mist rarely reaching Pollard where he stood high atop the quarterdeck. He leaned on the port rail, studying the lofty heights of two volcanoes that dominated the eastern horizon, farther out to sea. Ghost Island. He had never set foot on its mist shrouded shores, but from what he had heard of its inhospitable climate, the large island was aptly named.

"All clear!" Came the call from high atop the mainmast crow's nest.

Safely through the treacherous strait separating the outer reaches of the Undying Wall and the lava reefs surrounding Ghost Island, the captain of the *Crusher* left his place beside the helmsman and joined Pollard. "Quite a spectacular sight, eh Master Banebridge?"

"Aye." Pollard flexed his back muscles—the ship's railing not built for someone of his size. "You think anyone lives out there?"

The captain pulled on his short, pepper-grey beard. "Tough to say. Doubt it. Never seen any sign of life when sailing this way. I've always wanted to put in a lander and check out the island, but I've never gotten around to it."

"Someday, perhaps." Pollard leaned on the railing and smiled. Captain Bennek Crow had been sailing his father's ships for as long as Pollard remembered. Bennek had been a wiry, shrewd young sailor while Pollard had grown up in Storms End. The man hadn't spared much time for the son of Thoril Half-Hand, although Bennek had never been anything but fair during Pollard's youth. If anything, the good captain had hardened Pollard to the unforgiving ways of the sea—his teachings enlighten Pollard about the inherent dangers of the ocean and the men who sailed it.

"Aye." Bennek's gruff voice bore no trace of humour. "Perhaps the crew will bury me there when the time comes."

Pollard nodded. "Certainly a peaceful spot to spend out your days."

Bennek reached up to pat Pollard on the shoulder. "Get some rest, Master Banebridge. Judging by the rising seas, we've a hard trip ahead."

"Thanks, Cap. I'll head below shortly."

Bennek held his gaze for a moment, as if wanting to say something else. He flashed a quick smile and walked away—his sailor's swagger absorbing the roll of the ship.

Pollard watched the captain's progress as he disappeared down the steep steps emptying onto the main deck. Settling his elbows on the railing, he stared at the distant volcano—his mind hundreds of leagues north of their present position.

He had sent his most trusted advisor ahead on the *Half-Hand*—named after his father—the second of three warships in his family's possession. If anyone could ascertain the truth about the rogue thief preying upon the more affluent residents of Storms End, Lozen was the one for the job.

Pollard

Lozen, a proud warrior from the Altirius Mountains, had agreed to take leave of her tribe to help Pollard train selected members of the Splendoor Catacombs Guard in the way of her native people. She did this to honour the memory of Pollard's grandfather. Her way of paying homage to Thoril the Kraidic Crusher for his role in keeping her peoples free.

With the exception of his father, Pollard valued Lozen's counsel above all others. She possessed an uncanny knack of seeing past a person's persona to discover their true spirit. To Pollard, Lozen was much more than a medicine woman and warrior to her people. Lozen was a dear friend.

Pollard grunted. As conscientious as he was about morality and scruples, his gruff personality didn't lend itself to making friends easily. It took something special for someone to be the recipient of his friendship, but once earned, he would fight to the death to defend them.

The mission he had sent Lozen on left him reeling with mixed emotions. To quell an unfounded fear, he may have inadvertently placed her in danger. Should the Storms End Watch become suspicious of her true intentions, the captain of the Watch, Danth Emerald, wouldn't hesitate to kill her for her deception.

Pollard's father had messaged him through Master Pul of the Songsbirth Council, bringing to his attention a young woman who might prove to be a real boon to the Catacombs Guard. He had called her the Storms End Lightning Bolt—a person who had eluded Danth Emerald and his lackeys for years.

The Storms End Watch had placed the Lightning Bolt high on their wanted list. Though a thief by interpretation of the law, Thoril had insisted there was something special about the rogue lock pick; claiming he had it on good authority that she was merely doing what the city council would not. Looking after its vulnerable citizens.

Thoril feared that one day soon, the upstart woman would slip up. When she did, Danth's vigilante sense of justice would spell her untimely death.

Pollard bit his lower lip. He had purposely put his most faithful friend in harm's way in hopes of keeping a lawbreaker from being captured. Until he could return to Storms End, Lozen would have to find a way to cope on her own.

His distant gaze took in the receding volcanic peaks of Ghost Island as he reflected on his father's prophecy. If Thoril's words were true, the coming storm would fall upon Zephyr's people with the fiery fury of an erupting volcano.

Available now!

Keeper of the Jewel, book 1 in the Highcliff Guardians

Something dark is creeping across the elven kingdom of South March. Something so sinister, that if it is allowed to thrive unchecked, will lead to the end of dragonkind and quite possibly the termination of life as a whole.

The only thing standing in the way of the pervasive evil is a privileged young woman who wants nothing to do with her high standing in life, nor the oppressive responsibilities that accompany the title: Heir to the Willow Throne.

Book 2—Dragon Sect: Coming late 2021

To keep up with everything going on in the Soul Forge Universe, please visit my website at:
www.richardhstephens.com

All books are written within the Soul Forge Universe. There are two, loosely written stand-alone prequels, that I published first so I could understand the publishing side of writing. Though loosely written, fans enjoy the back stories about the main characters in the Soul Forge Saga.

The Royal Tournament:
Of Trolls and Evil Things:

I offer personalized, signed, paperback copies, complete with bling!

A discount is offered on the purchase of a trilogy.

If you wish to order: richardhstephens1@gmail.com

Books by Richard H. Stephens

Soul Forge - The Epic Fantasy Trilogy

Soul Forge – Book 1

Haunted by the murder of his family, a forgotten hero embarks upon a perilous quest fraught with demons both real and imagined.

Silurian Mintaka only wants another drink, but when the people of Zephyr need someone to save them from an evil sorcerer, he agrees to put aside his bitterness and wreak his revenge. Deception, betrayal, and fantastic beasts stand in his way. With the fate of the kingdom in the hands of a homicidal lunatic, the only thing left to do is pray.

Wizard of the North –Book 2

What do you get when you disturb a 500-year-old spirit who is in charge of protecting an ancient magic?

A death-defying flight to the heart of a serpent's nest.

If pulling a man through the flames wasn't enough, the highest wizard in the land detonates a thousand years of magical lore.

Not sure whether the king survived the firestorm, the people are left with little choice but to place their trust in a corrupt bishop.

A beast is unleashed and the kingdom's future lies in the hands of an eclectic band of companions who have lost their way.

Can an upstart mage, who isn't what they appear, stand against the evil sweeping the realm?

Into the Madness –Book 3

The epic conclusion of the Soul Forge Saga.

How do you survive a confrontation with a wyrm bent on destroying the world? Walk into its gaping maw and fight it from within.

A ragtag group of assassins set out to end the land's suffering only to discover death awaiting them with open arms.

A carefully hidden truth is revealed—the key to the kingdom's salvation if the Wizard of the North and her unstable companion can live long enough to unlock its secret.

Waylaid by an eccentric necromancer, and suffering a tragic loss that threatens to ruin their poorly laid plan, the companions stagger toward a fate no one ever envisioned.

An obsidian nightmare is summoned and Zephyr will never be the same.

Legends of the Lurker Series

Reecah's Flight –Book 1

Everyone knows dragons are dangerous, but to hunt them is insane.

There is something strange about the woman living on top of the hill and the people of Fishmonger Bay leave her alone. At least until the day she visits the village witch.

One magic user is bad enough; the emergence of another—intolerable.

Spinning out of control, Reecah must decide whether to slay the dragon or risk becoming a victim of her people.

Can Reecah find the key to unlock her family heritage or will she fall prey to the secret so many have died to protect?

Reecah's Gift – Book 2

The appalling mannerisms of those entrusted to protect the kingdom are shocking.

Braving the perils of a cutthroat city isn't what Reecah envisioned when she sought out a better place.

Can a ruthless giant equip her with the skills she needs to confront the king, or will his unorthodox ways end up being the death of her dreams?

Is an alliance with a murderous elf and a sly dwarf the best way to avert the plight of the dragons? And what is this *Gift* everyone seems to know about?

Everyone, except Reecah. Find out how the machinations of the evil prince and a traitorous wizard turn Reecah's quest on its head in this epic, second installment of the Legends of the Lurker series.

Reecah's Legacy – Book 3

The culmination of the Legends of the Lurker trilogy.

Reecah Windwalker comes into her own as she finds peace with her past and bravely sets out to fulfill her legacy.

Keeping a promise to a dead witch, Reecah seeks those who can help her learn the ways of her dragon magic as she embarks on a desperate journey to save the last of the dragons from the dark heir.

The races come together, but their combined strength may not be enough to prevent the high king's dragon slayers from eradicating the beauty from the land.

Banebridge Companion Novels

Larina – Book 1

(A story from the Soul Forge Universe)

Growing up on the streets of Storms End, Larina knows the only way to survive is to take matters into her own hands.

Skulking about the seedy alleyways and taverns of a once great city that has fallen from grace, survival has become a game of steal and lie, or die.

Larina uses her ill-begotten abilities to help the vulnerable, less fortunate souls abandoned by life. An act that fills her with a sense of purpose and pride.

That all changes when the man with the black warhammer comes to town. Now the Storms End Lightning Bolt must decide whether those she has fought so hard to protect will be better off if she ends up dead.

Sadyra – Book 2

(A story from the Soul Forge Universe)

Living in the shadows to avoid the brutality of parents harbouring a dark secret, Sadyra must force a violent confrontation if she is to keep her younger sisters from harm's way.

Begrudgingly accepted to work alongside a hardened group of sailors, Sadyra learns how to survive in a ruthless world.

To save her sisters from a fate worse than death, Sadyra goes against everything she feels is right, and life as she knows it will never be the same.

The Royal Tournament

(A story from the Soul Forge Universe)

The Royal Tournament has at long last come to the village of Millsford. For Javen Milford, a local farm boy, the news couldn't be better.

Finally, Javen can perform his chores on the homestead and partake in the biggest military games in the Kingdom, hoping beyond hope that just maybe, he might catch the eye of the king.

Javen enters the kingdom's flagship tournament only to discover that in order to win, one must be prepared to die.

Of Trolls and Evil Things

The (standalone) prequel to the Soul Forge Saga series!

Travel down an ever-darkening path where two orphans battle to survive upon a perilous mountainside, evading the predators and prowlers preying upon its slopes, and within its catacombs.

When the dangers they face force them from their mountain home, they end up in the cutthroat streets of Cliff Face plying their hands as beggars to survive.

Born in Simcoe, Ontario, in 1965, I began writing circa 1974; a bored child looking for something to while away the long, summertime days. My penchant for reading The Hardy Boys led to an inspiration one sweltering summer afternoon when my best friend and I thought, 'We could write one of those.' And so, I did.

As my reading horizons broadened, so did my writing. Star Wars inspired a 600-page novel about outer space that caught the attention of a special teacher who encouraged me to keep writing.

A trip to a local bookstore saw the proprietor introduce me to Stephen R. Donaldson and Terry Brooks. My writing life was forever changed.

At 17, I left high school to join the working world to support my first son. For the next twenty-two years I worked as a shipper at a local bakery. At the age of 36, I went back to high school to complete my education. After graduating with honours at the age of thirty-nine, I became a member of our local Police Service, and worked for 12 years in the provincial court system.

In early 2017, I retired from the Police Service to pursue my love of writing full-time. With the help and support of my lovely wife Caroline and our five children, I have now realized my boyhood dream.

If you wish to keep up to date on new releases, promotions and giveaways, please subscribe to my newsletter by checking out the contact tab on my website.

www.richardhstephens.com

Facebook:	richardhughstephens
Twitter:	RHStephens1
Instagram:	richard_h_stephens
YouTube:	bit.ly/2NKpOhn

www.ingramcontent.com/pod-product-compliance
Ingram Content Group UK Ltd.
Pitfield, Milton Keynes, MK11 3LW, UK
UKHW020143250726
13967UKWH00002B/844